Missing Dad 2

Missing Dad

2. Twisted

J. Ryan

Matador
9 Priory Business Park,
Wistow Road, Kibworth Beauchamp,
Leicestershire. LE8 0RX
Tel: 0116 279 2299
Email: books@troubador.co.uk
Web: www.troubador.co.uk/matador
Twitter: @matadorbooks

ISBN 978 1788036 696

British Library Cataloguing in Publication Data.
A catalogue record for this book is available from the British Library.

Printed and bound in the UK by TJ International, Padstow, Cornwall
Typeset in 11pt Aldine401 BT by Troubador Publishing Ltd, Leicester, UK

Matador is an imprint of Troubador Publishing Ltd

Twisted

CHAPTER 1

Out Of My Head

I knew that the only person who might be able to help me find Dad was Monsieur. He was hardly going to stroll back into our lives with the police after him. But I kind of waited in a fever of expectation that we would see him again. Day followed day, and nothing. Each time I looked at the photo of Dad and Monsieur, I couldn't stop hearing Monsieur's words: *'Once, I worked with your father, Joe. Then everything changed.'* When I got sucked into the world of undercover drug running that was L'Étoile Fine Wines, I seemed to get closer to my dad. After Monsieur disappeared, I felt further away than ever.

I got given a warning about the underage driving. Grandad said it would have gone really badly if I hadn't turned in Leah Wilks. She went to jail for that hit and run. It made the national news, like our cliff climb. After that, school got quite a bit less awful. I was made captain of the Year 11 footie team; and I even got the odd B in Maths, which was really weird.

Then, five whole months after Becks and I crawled out of that hole, it started. I didn't expect it. Stuff happens to everyone, doesn't it? How long does it take to cram it into some cupboard in your head, lock the door and get on with your life?

I kept waking up in the dark. My chest would feel tight. I couldn't breathe. Like when those rocks were trying to crush us to pieces. Jack said I sometimes shouted out in my sleep. He could hear me, right through the wall. I dreamed about the claw-like grip of Leah Wilks' hands, and those bullets that came at me out of the night.

I got so tired, one day I fell asleep in a History lesson. As I opened my eyes, I saw Bertolini standing over me in his black coat. I could even smell the cigars. I just stared and stared until he turned back into Miss Parker, wearing this baggy black dress. All through the detention, I could still smell the cigars.

Four more detentions later, I was up in front of the Head. 'Once again, you're giving us cause for concern, Joe.' But as he droned on, all I could see was Detective Inspector Wellington's bald head and bushy eyebrows. And the Head Master isn't bald. As I closed the door of his office behind me, I realised what I'd been burbling: 'It wasn't me, Inspector.'

That's when the school phoned Mum. She took me to the doctor. He said it was probably pre-GCSE stress. Suggested I take more exercise. But I knew I was losing it, big time. Even Becks was getting annoyed at having to repeat things to me. She said I sometimes stared straight through her, like I was looking at someone else. I don't even remember doing that.

Then, Mum's French friends invited me and a mate to Aix-en-Provence for the half-term hol. Mum was well up for it. She must have been desperate by then. And as

I stood on the deck of the ferry with Becks, watching Portsmouth disappear, all I could think was that, for all kinds of reasons, I'd rather be going to France than anywhere else in the world.

Becks and I sat watching the horizon, and together we looked at the photo of my father. When Mum gave it to me, she never knew that the second man in the picture, with the grey eyes and the half-smile, could hold the key to finding her missing husband, Commander Julius Grayling. She still doesn't. How could I ever hold out such a cruel hope?

CHAPTER 2

Sixty Seconds

Twenty four hours later, we're sat in a sun-dappled cafe in the centre of Aix-en-Provence, and all the dark shadows are far behind us. Above us, tall plane trees interweave their branches to shade us from the baking midday sun; all around is the soft tinkling of these marble fountains, with statues that all seem to be different snapshots from the same Roman rave. Whether or not, they're definitely enjoying themselves.

'Why did you bring the photo?' Becks sips her orange juice, green eyes surveying the picture closely.

'I like to have it with me, that's all.'

She frowns in the bright sunlight. 'How old do you think your dad was then?'

'I don't know. I didn't want to ask Mum, it's just too painful for her.'

'But look at Monsieur – he's got dark hair in the pic, and it's completely silver now.'

'Doesn't mean he's that old – stuff can make your hair lose its colour, can't it?'

A young dude with shoulder-length dark hair brushes impatiently past our table, and Becks quickly slips the photo into her handbag. 'Weren't you going to do some catch-up while we're here?'

'I've been working on my French; haven't you noticed?' I look away, and watch the families strolling past in the sunshine on the Cours Mirabeau. They're all so well dressed. Even little kids look like they've just tumbled off a catwalk in this place. I shuffle my chair as far under the cafe table as I can, to hide my battered jeans. Mum gave me some dosh to buy new ones, and I just had to blow it on a computer game, didn't I?

'It's your Eng Lit you're supposed to be working on.'

'Chill, Becks. I'll catch up when we get back.'

'Twenty four hours after we get home, you'll be ready for that test?'

'Twenty four hours is a long time.'

'You'll be asleep for most of it.'

'I'm not like the rest of humanity. I'll be revising.'

'In your dreams!'

'No ...'

'When we get back to the Gautiers, you're going to do some work, Joe.' Becks puts down her empty glass. 'Let's go.'

It's because Becks sounds like my mum, and we've got into this ridiculous argument, and I hate my horrible jeans, that I don't move. So the clock carries on ticking, and we're still at the cafe. And something comes closer which we'd have missed completely, if I'd just got my stupid, stubborn butt off that chair when she said.

'I haven't finished my coffee. And they're taking us for a meal in Marseille tonight, remember? Look, tomorrow, give me two hours, and then ask me anything you like about Raymond Chandler ... '

'Antoine! Arrête-toi!'

A small boy in a miniature two-piece suit pelts past our table. An irate dad is in hot pursuit, his Gucci sunglasses slipping off his nose. Becks shunts her chair forward to let dad through. We watch as he and mum – who's even skinnier than Posh – ambush small boy by the entrance to the cafe. Then, Becks' attention is caught by something else. Thankful that the heat's off me, I bury my nose in my café au lait. I've drained the cup, when I look up. She's still staring in the same direction.

'What is it?'

'That woman. She was looking at us like we're some kind of freak show.'

'Where?'

'She's just leaving – there, blonde hair, cream leather jacket.'

I can see plenty of blonde heads, but no cream leather jacket. 'She probably just forgot her glasses and can't see a thing. Grandad stares like that when he's lost his. Looks really creepy.'

Becks still gazes into the crowd. 'Her eyes were such a pale blue ...'

I glance at my watch. 'C'mon, you're right, we'd better head back to the Gautiers'. I might just fit in an hour of 'The Big Sleep'.' I start to push my chair out from under the table, taking a quick look behind me. I don't want to reverse into any designer-wear French kids.

Becks relaxes as I call the truce. 'They're so cool, the Gautiers. Letting us do our own thing most of the ...' Her voice tails off and takes on a warning note. 'Joe, you've got that look again. What is it?'

My throat's so dry I can hardly get the words out. 'Tell me I'm not seeing him, Becks. Please.'

'Who? Who can you see?'

'Over there, by the fountain. That huge dude in the overcoat, talking to the young guy who just went past ...'

'So, there's a big guy in a black coat ... what about him?'

My stomach's churning. 'It looks like Bertolini ... again ... but it can't be, can it?' I stare hard at the black coat. But it doesn't turn into Miss Parker. I can't see Becks anymore. It's like a fog's come down over everything, except for the guy who looks like Bertolini. I can just about hear Becks' voice. It's trying to sound reassuring but it's scared. For me.

'I've never seen Bertolini, Joe. But you're right. It can't be him. Now let's go.'

She grabs my hand, but my whole body's gone rigid. The guy in the coat is waving his hands around, like he's having an argument. Then, as though he can feel my stare, he starts to turn. A bomb goes off in my head. 'Get into the Ladies, now!'

'Why?'

'He mustn't see you with me.'

Becks takes a deep breath. 'Joe, listen to me. You know you could be imagining things again.'

Her voice sounds like background babble behind the roaring in my brain. I try not to shout. 'If there's a window, try and get out that way, round the back. I'll catch you there ...'

9

'But …'

'GO, Becks!'

Throwing me a frightened look, she slides out of her chair and disappears into the cafe. Bertolini's hard dark eyes are looking straight at me. The young guy's turning, too. And now I know I've gone deeply, certifiably insane. I can see a Monsieur who's about my age. Dark eyes, rather than Monsieur's grey ones. A mane of black hair, instead of Monsieur's cropped silver. But the same face, with those chiselled cheekbones. Swaying, I grab the chair. Bertolini's face contorts into a scowl. He takes quick steps towards me. One hand goes to his coat pocket.

My legs find some energy at last. I tear myself away from those eyes and dash inside the cafe, looking wildly around for somewhere to hide. Instantly, everything goes quiet. All these eyes are on me as I stand there, sweating and shaking. There's a movement to my right, behind the bar. The barman is slowly picking up the phone.

Just outside the glass doors, Bertolini's huge black shape is motionless. There's no way out but past him. No other doors in the floor to ceiling windows. A quiet voice whispers through the roaring in my head. I charge at the window furthest from Bertolini, and bounce off it. Chairs scrape around me. A hand grabs my arm. I shake it off, stagger to my feet and pick up a table. Smash it into the window. Huge jagged panes shower to the floor as I throw myself through it. A woman screams, 'C'est un terroriste!'

Blindly, I run. Where is there a side street that will let me find Becks? I crash into someone. We both stagger together on the pavement, then reel back from each other. 'You!' The young Monsieur takes me in as though he knows me as surely as I feel I know him. The dark eyes in that pale face are blazing with hate. Stunned, I stare back at him.

Police sirens start to wail. I run on, swerving into the first right turn I find. The street's deserted. I take another right. A slight figure in white shorts and a red top is half-way out of a small window. Her legs kick madly as she pushes her way through. I sprint to try and catch her, but before I can get there she's toppled to the ground. Still crouching, Becks stares up at me. 'Your arm!'

I look at the gash. 'Must've been the window.'

'God, Joe, what's happened?'

'We've got to get out of here!' I pull her up, and we run as the sirens get closer.

'We can take a cab back to the Gautiers, can't we? It's getting late.'

The hot air is so dry in my throat, my voice comes out in a croak. 'We can't go back to the Gautiers.'

'What do you mean? We have to go back!'

'Not with Bertolini after us.'

She stops and glances around. 'We've got away, haven't we? If we just take a cab and go by the side streets …?'

'We can't risk leading Bertolini and his gun anywhere near the Gautiers.' I take another breath of the hot Provence air, sweat running down my face. 'And he's not the only one who's looking for me now.'

Becks stares. 'Not the police! I heard the sirens, but … what have you done, Joe?'

'I haven't done anything! I was just trying to get out of his way. Now they think I'm a terrorist. Come ON!'

But Becks just stands there, looking at me like she doesn't know me anymore. And it hits me like a brick in the head. 'You don't believe me, do you?'

She whispers, 'We left those shadows behind, in that hole. They're gone now, Joe.' She holds out her hand like I'm a little kid. 'Let's go back to the Gautiers. They must be getting worried.'

It's like that fog is still swirling between me and her. I try and find the words. 'You saw the dude in the black coat, didn't you? He was real?'

'Yes, I saw him. But it could have been anyone who'd just suddenly become Bertolini in your mind. Like Miss Parker did.'

Suddenly it all slots beautifully into place like Lego. Or is this the rock solid certainty that crazy people feel? 'But this time, he didn't change into anyone else. So it has to be Bertolini behind us.'

She's still hesitating when a cop car screams down the street just beyond. Her eyes meet mine. I say quickly, 'I'm not out of it anymore, Becks, believe me!' We throw ourselves into a doorway as the car shoots past, skids round a corner and disappears.

Becks peers out after it. 'What do we do now?'

We walk on quickly down the street. 'Get as far away from the Gautiers as possible.'

'Where? Home?'

'We can't go home either. Bertolini knows where I live – remember?'

'God, Joe, this is such a mess! The Gautiers will ring

your parents when we don't show up. Then they'll go mad with worry too!'

Sirens blare again, much too close. We slide into an alleyway. A police car screeches into our street. It blasts past, we wait a few seconds, then hurry on. I'm looking for signs out of Aix when Becks says, 'Who was the guy with Bertolini? I expect you know him as well.'

I can hear the sarcasm in her voice. I probably deserve it. 'I thought I did. But I've never seen him before in my life.' And with every step I take, that hate-filled face is in front of me, like I'm seeing a ghost.

CHAPTER 3

A Knife In The Dark

I'd forgotten how big Aix is. But in the earlier years when Mum took me and Jack, we never walked this far from the Gautiers. The sun sinks lower in the blue Provence sky, as we trudge mile after mile along side streets. Once, I lose my sense of direction completely, and realise that we're heading back into town. Every time a car approaches, I strain to see the driver. I keep hearing footsteps behind us, but when I turn around, there's no one there.

Becks pushes damp red hair out of her eyes. 'Can't we take a train … a bus?'

'The police will be looking for me on trains and buses.'

'What if we walk into a police station and explain that there's been an awful mistake?'

'Oh yeah, and they're going to believe that, aren't they? Like I bashed my way through a plate glass window by mistake? They'll probably think I'm on drugs as well as a terrorist.'

Becks goes quiet. I look at her tired face as she trudges beside me. And I stop suddenly. 'I'm an idiot.'

'What?'

'There's nothing to stop you going back to the Gautiers, Becks. The police didn't see you. I don't think Bertolini did either. I've got some Euros – you can get a cab …' I fish in my pocket for my wallet.

She gives me a pitying look. 'Know something? You really ARE an idiot.'

'You shouldn't be in this mess with me. Tell the Gautiers you don't know what happened … like, I just lost it, and disappeared …?'

Becks pulls her matted red hair up into a top knot, and marches off without a backward glance. 'You're so good at digging an even bigger hole for both of us!'

It's starting to get dark, as we walk down a small street with cobbled stones. The houses all have their wooden shutters closed. Now, it's the night, not the sun, that they're keeping out. A white cat sits in one of the doorways. As we pass, it mews softly, and I think of big, cuddly Fats at home on my pillow. My phone goes.

'Answer it, Joe!'

I try to sound casual, but my voice is still croaking. 'Hi, Mum.'

'Jean Paul called us, Joe. He's really worried that you and Becks haven't come back. What's going on?'

'We're fine, Mum. Can you just tell him that there was a police thing around the cafe where we were, and we'll be really late because they were stopping and searching people everywhere?'

'What police thing? You're not involved with it, are you?'

'It was nothing to do with me, Mum, honest.'

'So why can't you phone Jean Paul yourself?'

'Out of credit. I'll top up tomorrow, promise.'

'Get organised, Joe! We gave you plenty to take with you! Call us as soon as you get back to the Gautiers.'

'Yeah. Sorry. It's really great here, Mum. Thanks for everything.'

Becks darts me a look and mutters, 'Yeah, Mum, it's really great here!'

'You wait till your dad calls you.' Before the words are out of my mouth, I'm sorry I said them.

She shrugs. 'You know he never calls. It'll more likely be big bro. And then not for days.'

I could kick myself. Becks' parents split when she was ten years old, and she doesn't get on that well with her dad. Now her holiday's in ruins. And I don't have a plan. I'm being a total asshole.

The buildings are just silhouettes against the violet sky as we walk quickly on through the dimly-lit streets. Then Becks stops. 'What's that? Some kind of weird graffiti?'

Painted on the grey wall of the building opposite is a huge image of a heart with an arrow through it. Blood's coming from it, in two large red teardrops on the battered stones. A sign below says, 'Le Sacré Coeur'. 'I think it's a church.'

'It's horrible.'

We're staring at the ghoulish image when we hear the sirens and the roaring engine. 'The churchyard – quick!'

We scramble over the wall, while tyres scream and headlamps blaze into the street. In front of us is a large tombstone, with a fierce-looking stone angel on it, hand raised, telling intruders to back off. We throw ourselves

16

down behind it. A huge swarm of insects lifts off from the dry grass, and buzzes round our heads.

'Eeugh!' Becks flaps them away from her face.

'Shhh!'

The police car stops, doors open, and feet pound on the cobbles. Then we hear a loud banging, and shouts of 'Ouvrez! Police!'

Her whisper comes through the shadows. 'Joe …'

'It's alright, I don't think it's us they're after.'

The door of the house opens, feet thump inside, and the door bangs shut. Some sort of argument is going on, but I can't understand what they're saying. 'Let's get moving.'

Becks' voice is tiny. 'There's a snake on my hand.'

I peer at her hand, rigid in the grass. I can just make out a slim tail lying across her wrist. We watch, holding our breath, as the small snake raises its head, and a tongue flickers out, testing the air, and the company. I can't see the markings in the twilight. Even if I could, I wouldn't know if it was poisonous, or just a harmless grass snake. The snake starts a slow, coiling journey up her bare arm.

'Stay really still, Becks.'

Her voice is as shaky as mine. 'I can't … not for much longer.'

I think frantically back to my PE lessons, where you have to be so fast throwing a cricket ball, you turn four movements into one. I get a bead on the snake as it steadily moves up her arm. Then my hand arcs, I grab the smooth body, the head twists swiftly towards my fingers and I hurl it into the grass. We race towards the wall of the churchyard, slide back over it and run till we're three streets away.

My throat's burning in the stifling air. We slow down, gasping for breath, sweat trickling down our faces. 'There's a sign to the North. We're still heading out of town.'

We plod on. Becks keeps looking sideways at me, like she wants to say something. Then she just looks away again. If only we'd left that cafe when she said.

A mouth-watering smell of beef in wine hits us as we come up to a restaurant. At the tables outside, families are eating and chatting in the warm night. Little kids, grannies, mums and dads, all sit together. Chunks of baguette are being dipped into plates with juicy meat in that fragrant sauce. With a dull shock, I think about the Gautiers. We should be sitting in a restaurant in Marseille with them now. They must be horrified that we haven't come back, even if Mum has managed to get through to them. Have they called the police? And been told I'm a wanted terrorist? We walk slowly past the tables, where friendly faces look up and wish us 'Bonsoir, Monsieur, Mademoiselle!'

A few paces past the restaurant, Becks stops. Her eyes are imploring, as she wipes long strands of hair off her face. 'Can't we at least call the Gautiers? Tell them we're OK?'

'I don't know how we can, Becks. Not without having to tell them everything, and worrying them even more.'

She looks longingly at the restaurant, then at me. 'Mightn't it be safe to go back now, Joe? There's been no sign … has there?'

The memories crowd in. 'There never was a sign. Then, he was there. Right behind me. With that gun. If we go back, we could end up with his hit man outside the Gautiers' place this time, just like my family's house then. I can't bring that down on them, Becks, can I?'

She shudders, remembering. 'No. It was horrible.'

I watch her dejected figure as she starts walking again. She bought those white shorts and the red top specially for this trip. She was so excited, because she'd never been to France before, even though she's way better than me at French. I can feel a stinging at the back of my eyes as I hurry after her. 'Becks …'

She turns, with a look of hope. 'Yes?'

'I'm so sorry … about all this …'

The hope fades into disappointment as she slips her hand into mine. 'It's not your fault, Joe. But it's scary, being on the run and nowhere to go.'

'I know.'

'And I'm so thirsty.'

At least that's one thing I can fix. I dash into the restaurant and come out with a large bottle of Evian. 'Sorry they didn't do chocolate.'

'Stop saying sorry!'

—⚏—

Half an hour later, we leave Aix behind us, and start to trudge along the narrow track that passes for a hard shoulder on the A51 North. I'm still trying to make a plan, but I'm so tired, my brain isn't working. Huge lorries with trailers blast by, so fast they almost drag us into their slipstream, flashing us with their massive racks of headlamps, and hooting like we have no right to be here on foot. We probably don't. Becks shouts above the roar of the traffic, 'Can't we try and hitch a lift?'

'Can you imagine one of these monsters even seeing us? Anyway, I'm not sure if the thumb up thing works outside the UK.'

'What do you mean?'

'It could be like the worst insult I could throw at this truckie's mum or daughter or sister. I know it's that way in Sicily, or somewhere.'

We've been walking for another half hour, when she says quietly, in a pause between the flashing headlamps and screaming engines, 'The young guy, Joe, that Bertolini was talking to?'

'What about him?'

'You said you thought you knew him, but you'd never seen him before. What made you say that?'

There's a roaring behind us. Another convoy of huge trucks is on the way. I turn and look at her strained face, as the headlamps light it more and more brightly. The noise becomes deafening. I shout, 'He reminded me of Monsieur …'

Suddenly, brakes shriek. A cloud of dust and gravel flies up just a few hundred yards behind us. One of the trucks veers crazily onto the track we're on, then swerves back towards the carriageway. More brakes scream, and horns blast. We throw ourselves out of the way. Still weaving around, the artic thunders past, showering us with stones.

Becks scrambles up, her voice unsteady. 'I can't take

this anymore. I'm going back!' She dashes away into the dark.

'Becks!' I drag myself up and follow her, hating these beasts with their blinding lights and horrible noise. 'Becks!!' Headlamps blaze into my face. I keep stumbling. I can't see a thing in the glare.

Out of the darkness, her hand grabs my arm. 'I saw something!'

'What?'

'It was like a shadow, down there on the track …'

Wordlessly, we turn and run. And it's anger that's firing the energy in my legs now. A fury that something could have dared to creep up behind Becks in the dark. I slip my arm round her back and almost lift her off the ground as we fly up the track.

My mobile goes again. I wrestle it out of my pocket. Deafened by the roaring trucks, I wonder if my ears are playing tricks. It sounds like the voice we last heard in a cave room that was about to go up in fire and smoke forever, five long months ago. 'Joe, where are you?'

'Monsieur …?'

Becks takes quick glances behind us as we run.

'Joe, you MUST tell me where you are! Your life depends on it.'

I shout, in between gasps, 'We're on the A51 out of Aix … going north. We've just … passed a sign … Vauvenargues.'

'You must stay by the sign, but get right out of sight. I will be there in twenty minutes.'

As I shut down the call, Becks grabs my arm like she's about to tear it out of its socket. She drags me across the dual carriageway to the central barrier. Now we're in the middle of yowling trucks going both ways, with just a few feet of dried grass between them and us. Her voice is tight with fear. 'It wasn't a shadow!'

We wait for a split-second break between the roaring monsters, then run like hell across the South-bound lanes. As more trucks scream past, we dive into the hedge beside the track. Thorns dig into our skin like claws. On the other side, the field is almost total darkness, lit only by the passing lights of the traffic.

Becks whispers, 'How long till Monsieur gets here?'

'Twenty minutes.'

'Then we have to keep moving!'

The ground is rutted and dry from the Provence heat. We stumble as we move further into the blackness of the field. I look behind, straining to hear if we're still being followed. What if our pursuer has a torch that will suddenly pick us out like helpless targets? We've got to find some cover.

Becks hisses, 'Listen!'

Heavy feet are coming towards us. In the flashing lights of the traffic, we can see large, bulky shapes. Then I hear this wet, snuffly breathing. 'It's only cows.'

'They've got horns, Joe!'

And at last, I've got an idea. 'Follow me, very quietly. They're probably just young bullocks. We might have found a place to hide.'

We walk slowly towards the cattle. They stop dead, heads swinging towards us with curiosity. 'Stand still now, Becks.'

As soon as we stop, they start to approach us again,

snuffling and huffing, until their huge, warm bodies surround us completely. A heavy hoof comes down near my foot. I whip it away. Then, a large, rasping tongue licks my face. It's like having a shave without any gel. The minutes tick by. I glance at my watch. Thirteen still to go. 'You alright, Becks?'

'If they'd stop licking my hair.'

Just as she says that, the bullock that was taking the skin off my face throws his head in the air and lets out a bellow like a ship's fog horn. Suddenly, there's pounding hooves and snorting breath all around us. Huge bodies thunder past, kicking great lumps of mud over us. Headlights glint on the curved horns. Something smashes into my back like a rocket launcher. I fly through the air and crash land. I daren't move, watching their bellies as they jump over me. The ground shakes as heavy hooves plough into the earth, inches from my face.

Then, the thundering hooves start to fade into the distance. Still lying on my stomach, I look around for Becks in the darkness. She's crouched motionless beside me. She whispers, 'I … think we know what spooked the cattle.'

I'd thought it was the growling of the traffic. I can't see how many dogs are surrounding us. But the deep gurgle in their throats says they're big. A snarl erupts inches from my hand, and I want to snatch it away. Towering over us, lit by the passing headlamps, is an enormous, gaunt hound. I can hear his panting breath. It stinks worse than Bertolini's, as his saliva drips onto my hand.

What easy targets we are now for whoever's

following us. There can't be more than a few minutes left before Monsieur gets to that sign for Vauvenargues. Where we won't be, unless we can think of something. The growling continues, for minutes that feel like hours. Then, a wet muzzle touches my hand. I wait for sharp teeth and iron jaws. Or a bullet out of the dark.

Suddenly, my mobile goes again. Powerful jaws snap shut right next to my fingers, as I drag the phone out of my pocket. I'm about to hurl it away into the field to get them off us, when I have a better idea. As the snarling gets louder, I wrench off one of my trainers, and chuck it in a giant lob as far away as I can. In a howling mob, the dogs launch themselves after it. Becks and I race back to the hedge. More thorns rip at our skin as we fight our way through.

'It's got my hair!'

Thorns stab into my hands like poisoned needles as I tear off the branch that's caught her.

Scrambling out of the hedge, we look quickly from side to side and make another suicidal dash across the lanes. The sign for Vauvenargues is a hundred yards to our left. Just as we get there, a blaze of headlamps dazzles us. The car shoots past, then brake lights go on, and tyres sing. It's a Merc sports convertible, hood up. I grab Becks' hand, and we run for it, tripping and stumbling, legs like lead.

The door's open, waiting. We throw ourselves into the back seat, and I slam the door behind us. The driver floors the throttle. As we shoot onto the carriageway, there's a ripping sound, a dull thud and a muffled cry. Becks is crammed as tiny as she can get into the corner of the seat. She's staring at a bright knife. It's gone clean through the canvas roof, and into the driver's head rest.

It's then that I realise. Whoever was chasing us didn't bother to follow us into the field. He waited, by the sign to Vauvenargues. Because it wasn't us he wanted to kill tonight.

CHAPTER 4

The Lost Son

'Keep down! That may not be the only incident before we are all in a safer place.' Monsieur's eyes never leave the rear view mirror as we hurtle along. I reach for the knife, and gingerly pull it out of the head rest. Becks and I stare at the gleaming blade that was following us all that way in the dark, looking for Monsieur. I shove it under the seat.

We must have gone about twenty miles at more than a hundred miles an hour. The Merc dodges and weaves effortlessly around those huge trucks. Then Monsieur takes a right off the A51 onto a minor road, and shortly after, a left onto a rough track. We slow down, as the headlamps shine on tall, wrought-iron gates, with high stone walls reaching into the night either side. He hits a switch on the dashboard, and the gates swing silently open, closing behind us as we drive through.

'Awesome!' Becks stares out of the car window, as lights like large cats-eyes gleam on, either side of the gravel driveway. I catch a faint glimpse of lawns around us, with statues and fountains.

The Merc stops, and I can make out a stone porch with a solitary light hanging in it. Above it, the dark shape of a huge chateau rises into the night sky. Only three windows have lights on; two on the ground floor, and one on the floor above. Monsieur turns off the engine. He's looking ahead of him, not at the ancient building, or at us. 'Welcome to L'Étoile, my friends.'

He slips from the driving seat, a shadow with silver-gleaming hair. We scramble out of the Merc and follow, our feet crunching on the gravel. I can't hear Monsieur's feet. Thinking back, I'm not sure I ever have. He's always had a footfall like a panther.

The wooden door inside the porch is carved with an intricate star, radiating sixteen points of light. I whisper to Becks, 'It's the same as the image in L'Étoile Fine Wines' logo.' We gaze at the beams, so finely crafted that they reflect the light from the porch lamp.

As we approach, the door opens slowly, and we can see the silhouette of a tiny figure. The chic old lady who greeted me on the day of my job interview with Monsieur holds out her hand.

'Madame de L'Étang …?'

She looks as severe as she did on that first day, but she takes my hand warmly. 'Sois le bienvenu, Joe. Ton amie, aussi.'

I get as big a shock as I did that night outside the room with the chandeliers, when I discovered that Monsieur really was French, after all my clever traps to try and prove that he wasn't. Now, Madame is speaking perfect French too. I realise that there's so much I don't know about Monsieur, it could choke a black hole.

He waves us inside, towards a room off the hallway. 'Vous avez faim?'

Becks nods eagerly. 'Oui, Monsieur, merci!' Madame scuttles away, just like she did on that morning when my eventful career as a drug-running chauffeur all began.

Monsieur is as immaculately dressed as ever. Still the Armani suit. He's almost the same as he was when I first met him, and thought to myself that I wouldn't mind looking like him when I got to his age. But his face is drawn and tired. It can't have been easy for him over the last five months, with the police after him; and now, an assassin. How did he know we were out there, with that knife behind us?

The room has a high ceiling, with chandeliers like the ones in Monsieur's office in Bristol. But these chandeliers have no light. There are rugs on the polished wood floor, an antique desk, and ornate wooden tables; like the ones in the cave below the cave, where we found Monsieur before the explosions began.

He gestures to me and Becks to make ourselves comfortable on a sofa that's loaded with cushions. I look at my arms, all streaked with blood from the glass and thorns; Becks frantically picks twigs out of her hair. 'We're a pair of tramps, Monsieur!'

He shakes his head, the half-smile there again at last. 'It does not matter. Sit down, both of you. You must be exhausted.'

He sits opposite us, next to a huge fireplace with carved stonework around it, where no fire burns. Only some small table lamps cast a gentle glow on the walls, with their many portraits and photographs.

Monsieur's grey eyes look directly at mine, and it

feels like that job interview the first time I met him. 'How did you come to be in Aix, Joe?'

'Me and Becks were on holiday, staying with friends of my mum. I've been to Aix before, we've known the Gautiers for years.'

'And today, you saw someone, didn't you?'

'Big Head … I mean, Bertolini. He was the one who shot at me, wasn't he, Monsieur? I've been wanting to ask you for so long!'

'We will come to that. Who else did you see, Joe?'

'I saw someone … who looked like you. But he was like, my age.'

Monsieur looks into the darkness of the unlit fireplace. He's seeing images there that we can't. 'When our son was born to us, Lisette and I felt that our life together was just beginning. Arnaud was to be our future … and the future of L'Étoile.'

Madame brings in a tray with soup, bread and mineral water. Monsieur thanks her, and she disappears with her tapping feet. Oblivious of the food, we just watch Monsieur, and listen. He continues, no emotion in his quiet voice. 'Soon after Arnaud was born, Lisette became seriously ill. It was … not possible to save her.'

I feel a kind of shock, because I'd thought he was going to say that something terrible happened to his son, not his wife.

'Arnaud grew up to be a child who never cried. At school, his exam results were exceptional.'

'What subjects did he enjoy most, Monsieur?'

He replies, with a slight smile at the memory, 'Arnaud loved languages. He could speak English, German and

Italian like a native. He would read Latin out loud like a Roman. He seemed to love Latin the most, the dead language.'

Becks softly asks the question that's been eating at me, but there was no way I knew how to say it. 'Monsieur, you've been speaking about Arnaud in the past tense, as though he's dead, like the Latin he loved so much. But, Monsieur, Arnaud isn't dead, is he?'

Monsieur looks back into the empty fireplace, his voice almost a whisper now. 'I was not a good father to Arnaud after Lisette died. I couldn't think about the pain of a child who has lost his mother. I thought only about my own grief. I couldn't forgive myself ...'

He pauses. 'Over the years after Lisette's death, slowly, Arnaud and I grew apart. He made new ... friends. It must have been when he was only fourteen that he started to take the drugs. I only found out afterwards, when it was too late. Arnaud was getting his cocaine from a contact who was working for Alfredo Bertolini.'

'Bertolini!' Becks hisses out the word. She's making the same connections as I am.

Monsieur's voice is iron-cold, now. 'Bertolini took a great interest in Arnaud, because he saw an opportunity. L'Étoile Fine Wines was a well-respected family business that had been trading in Bristol for more than a hundred years. He laid his plans very carefully. He started to draw Arnaud towards him. Giving my son the kind of attention that I ... did not. He also gave Arnaud money, the good life. Anything he wanted.'

Monsieur leans forward, towards the fire that isn't

there beneath that carved stone mantelpiece. He's seeing those ghosts again. Now, we can see them too.

'When I first met Bertolini, it was already a fait accompli. He came to me one day with a proposition that he knew I could not refuse. I think you know what that proposition was, Joe.'

In the lamplight, I see his eyes flash with anger remembered. I feel his anger too, as the final pieces of the puzzle start to drop into place. 'He wanted to use L'Étoile Fine Wines as a cover for his drug running, didn't he? Everything would go on as before, so it wouldn't attract any attention. But you weren't going to be Le Directeur anymore, were you, Monsieur? Only in name. And you had to agree, because Bertolini had taken your son like a kind of hostage. He could have killed Arnaud at any time. It would just have looked like a drugs overdose.'

Monsieur is very still. All I can see is the light reflecting off that short silver hair, and glinting in his grey eyes. I can't even hear Becks breathing. In the soft glow of the lamplight, she could be a statue on this sofa.

'Now, you may ask me all those other questions that are in your mind, Joe.'

'Was it Bertolini who shot at me on the run back from London that night? And again, coming back from Birmingham?'

'It was Bertolini.'

'Then …. why?'

We can hear the revulsion in Monsieur's calm voice. 'Bertolini doesn't do drugs himself. He doesn't need them. He gets his fix from inflicting pain. He is completely addicted to the sensation of power over the powerless.

He had recruited teenage boys before, Arnaud's age like yourself, to L'Étoile Fine Wines, as my chauffeur. Then, he would destroy them, to remind me that he still had Arnaud in his control. The last one to get arrested for drug running was a young man called Jamie Johnson.'

I feel a stab of recognition. Lenny's brother, who he told me was in jail, 'fitted up'. Lenny knew who Jamie was working for when he was arrested. No wonder he warned me not to apply for the job.

'I know Jamie's brother.'

'Jamie was lucky. He wasn't shot, like you so nearly were. But he was sent to prison for something he didn't do.'

'Then, it was my turn?'

'You had threatened Bertolini; delivered one of his drivers to the police. So it must have been a double pleasure for him, to bring you under his control, and give you the illusion that you were in a dream job. Then, shoot at you, when you had a car boot full of cocaine.'

My mind is rewinding the tape so fast now. 'That night in London … Bertolini … he seemed sort of jumpy. Was it because of what Madame said later, about a security scare? Was he afraid of a rival gang?'

Monsieur says simply, 'No. He was afraid of me.'

He gets up, with a restless movement, and stands with his back to the carved stone fireplace, the anger still an undercurrent in his quiet voice. 'When you were sent on that run to Kensington, Bertolini had told me that it would be your last. He was tired of his latest possession. It was time to complete his act of revenge on you, for daring to challenge him in the way you had done.'

Monsieur's eyes are somewhere else, like he's replaying the scene in his mind. 'When he said to me that night that you would be next, I told him that it was going to stop – the killing, the drugs, the lies. It was over, his hold on me that had for so long made me nothing more than his slave.'

Ton empire est foutu, c'est tout. I remember those words I overheard in the room with the chandeliers.

Becks whispers, 'Weren't you afraid of what he could do to Arnaud?'

Monsieur's voice is steady. 'I have never ceased to fear for Arnaud, Mademoiselle. But I could not continue to be part of this obscenity.'

I can see Monsieur in that underground room now. We're sat opposite him, just before that first awful bang. 'So, who blew up the building? Was it Bertolini, trying to get rid of everything, because he knew the police were all round the place?'

Monsieur's reply is just as calm as before. 'No, Joe. I laid the explosives. I meant it, when I said to him that it was all going to stop.'

So Becks guessed correctly. But still I stare at Monsieur, with this aching question. 'When we crashed in on you, just before it all went up – why were you still there, Monsieur?'

He walks slowly around the room, stopping next to a framed portrait, and touches it gently. White lace cascading down her shoulders, a long white dress for her wedding day, the young woman is so beautiful that Becks and I just stare like idiots. The bridegroom with his arm round her waist, and such pride in his eyes, is the young

33

man with the black hair who I saw this afternoon. But the eyes are grey, not brown.

Monsieur moves on, like he's sleepwalking almost, to another picture. It's a little boy, maybe seven or eight, grinning cheekily at the camera, with a rush of dark hair, and brilliant brown eyes saying, 'Look at me, I'm special.'

Like he's waking from a dream, Monsieur turns away from the picture to us. 'Arnaud has belonged to Bertolini for a long time, now. I still love him more than anyone else in this world. But I fear that I can never regain his love. He must feel that I rejected him forever, after Lisette died. Bertolini has stepped into my place, fostering Arnaud's deadly habit, and encouraging him to reject me in turn. To hate me. You saw what happened tonight.'

'Are you saying you think it was Arnaud following us, Monsieur? It was Arnaud who threw the knife?'

Monsieur replies, with a quiet simplicity that makes my skin crawl, 'Arnaud texted me this evening. He'd seen you, Joe, in Aix. He has an apartment there, when he's not in Corsica at Bertolini's mansion, or in his Bristol house. The text said, he was going to enjoy putting a knife in your back.'

'But … it was you he wanted …?'

'So you see, I really did not have anything more to lose, that afternoon in Bristol.'

I remember Monsieur in that cave room, embracing me like a long-lost son. Telling me that he owed me his life.

'What WERE you going to do Monsieur, before we arrived?'

'It is of no consequence now, Joe.' His grey eyes

look directly at mine again. 'But perhaps you would like to tell me how it was that the pair of you appeared on the national news the next day, climbing the Avon Gorge?'

Monsieur sits down and listens, motionless, as we tell him in between mouthfuls of soup and bread how we ended up on the Gorge. His grey eyes have a look in them that I don't understand. Then he says, his voice just a whisper, 'You two came back into that burning office, copied all those files from the computer and then went through that hell? You came so close to death! Why in God's name did you do it?'

My mouth's full, so Becks jumps in. 'Detective Inspector Wellington was convinced it was you behind the drug running, Monsieur. We thought there might be something in those files that would prove it was Bertolini.'

'So you took them to the police?'

'Well, yes. We didn't want to see you go to prison for something you didn't do, Monsieur.'

I've never seen Monsieur's face look so grave. 'My young friends, your courage and your concern for me have placed you in danger far worse than those dreadful caves.'

He gets up and goes quickly across to the desk by the wall, below the photograph of the child Arnaud. Taking a pen, he writes quickly on a piece of note paper. Then he reaches into a drawer in the desk, pulls out a thick, sealed envelope and writes on that too.

Becks asks, 'What about Arnaud, Monsieur? How are you going to protect yourself from him? Or are you going to try and get him away from Bertolini, and back to you?'

Monsieur looks up from his writing, his voice as steady as ever. 'Whatever he has done, whatever he may yet do, I cannot have my own son hunted down like an animal. And one hint that I am trying to bring him back would be enough for Bertolini to destroy him.'

'So … you can't do anything, until …'

'Until Bertolini is behind bars.' He looks at us again and I still can't understand what's in his eyes. 'And one day, maybe he will be; thanks, perhaps, to that memory stick that you both risked your lives for. I will always be grateful to you for that.'

As he speaks, I can hear the words that Monsieur isn't saying. 'Even if it all comes to nothing.' He has no hope of ever seeing his son again. Dimly, in the darkest corner of my mind, a familiar voice says, 'We're going to get Arnaud back to you, Monsieur.' I look at Becks and it's like she's reading my thoughts. Her eyes connect with mine. We both know that Commander Julius Grayling would want us to help his long time friend.

Monsieur hands me the piece of paper. He's written down two addresses, both in Bristol. 'The Clifton address is where Arnaud stays when he is in England. It may help to avoid your paths crossing again. The second address is a deeply unfashionable terraced house in Knowle West. It's a place I sometimes use when I have no desire for anyone to know my whereabouts. You can go to ground there until this affair is over.'

I'm about to reply when he shakes his head slowly,

reaching again into the desk drawer. He hands me a key. 'You know you cannot go home again until this is finished, Joe. You too, now, Mademoiselle. Bertolini has many eyes that could be watching for your return. And he will have told Arnaud everything, don't forget.'

I slip the key and the piece of paper into my pocket. Then he passes me the envelope. 'You may also be in need of funds, until your lives can get back to normal.'

Madame comes in for the tray. Monsieur gestures towards her. 'It's time I introduced you. Madame Françoise de L'Étang is my brave and devoted aunt. She has always been at my side.'

We shake hands with Madame. She smiles at us again, looking at our ripped and bloody jeans. 'There are some clothes for you both upstairs, to make you a little more presentable for your journey back to England. Mademoiselle?' She ushers Becks out.

Monsieur hands me the landline. 'And now you must call your mother and your hosts, and tell them that you are safe, Joe.' He pauses. 'And you need to say why you will not be returning home for a while. I know that will not be easy for you.'

As he leaves the room, the phone feels heavy in my hand. What on earth am I going to say to Mum?

At the first ring, the receiver's snatched up. 'Joe, for heaven's sake, where are you?'

I can hear Jack's saxophone playing upstairs. Mum must be gripping the phone, and running a hand through her hair till it's going in all directions. I swallow hard. 'We had a call ... from some mates. They were like, camping in the Dordogne, and one of them's got into trouble with the police. They can't speak a word of French, so we've gone to help out.'

'You've WHAT?'

'They haven't got anyone else, Mum …'

'Do you have any idea how worried the Gautiers are? How could you do this?'

'I'm sorry …'

'Sorry isn't the right word, Joe. Your Grandad's going to come out and fetch you both home. And this is absolutely the last time that …'

'There's no need, honest. We'll be on our way back … tomorrow, maybe?'

'There are no 'maybe's' about this, Joe! Now where exactly are you?'

'Look, Mum, I can't tell you any more than that. But we can sort this on our own …' I can hear her talking quickly to Grandad as I stutter on.

'I'm putting your grandfather on the line. You'd better listen to him, even if you won't to me!'

'What's going on, Joe? Are you alright?' I can see Grandad's bewildered face as he shoves his glasses onto his head.

'We're both fine, Grandad. I'm really sorry that the Gautiers are so worried. And I know I've been a lousy guest, disappearing like that … but …'

'But what, Joe? What's happened?'

I take a deep breath. 'Grandad, have you ever been in a situation where a mate really needed your help? And it was like, more important than anything else?'

He hesitates. 'Well, yes. Once. But …'

'And could you tell anyone about it at the time?'

38

He sighs. 'I know where this is leading, Joe. You're asking us to trust you. No more questions, until you can tell us the answers. That's a pretty tough call, given the circumstances.'

'Yes, it is, Grandad. But will you? Please?'

'Give me a moment.' He's talking to Mum. She still sounds so angry. Grandad's voice is quiet. I catch the words '… remember how he coped the last time …'

'He's just a child, for God's sake!'

'He's had to deal with situations that most adults never could …'

Then there's a pause so long that I think we might have been cut off. Grandad must have put his hand over the mouthpiece. Finally, his voice is back. 'How long will this business take, Joe?'

'I'm sorry, but I don't know.'

'You have to be back in school when term starts. Even if you haven't sorted out your mate's problem. Do you understand that?'

'OK.'

'That gives you till a week tomorrow at the latest to come home.'

'Right.'

'This cuts both ways, Joe. We need you to promise that you'll be back by the Sunday.'

Eight days. 'I promise.'

'And if you hit trouble that you can't deal with, you must call us straight away. We need your promise on that too.'

'I will call, Grandad.'

After Grandad's rung off, I sit staring at the pictures on the wall. The child Arnaud looks back at me with bright, hopeful eyes. I whisper, 'I don't know how we're going to do this.'

'Do what?'

I jump. A slim young woman in a black shirt and black jeans is standing behind me. 'God, Becks – I didn't recognise you.'

'It's your turn now. Madame's put some clothes out for you upstairs. And trainers, so you won't have to do that weird hobble anymore.'

I hold out the phone. 'Are you going to call your dad?'

She shrugs. 'No point. He thinks I'm still living it up in Aix. Now hurry up and get changed – Monsieur says he can get us on the early morning flight from Marseille if we leave in five minutes.'

As I button the black shirt, it reminds me of my chauffeur's uniform. I haven't worn dark colours since that time. I didn't expect to again, except for a job interview, or a funeral. But then, I didn't expect to see Monsieur again, either. And now that we're with him again, I so wish I could ask him about Dad. But how can I when he's in this dark place?

He's waiting for me with Becks and Madame, at the bottom of the ornate staircase. Madame shakes our hands, then she hugs us, and her eyes are glistening. 'I hope we may meet again in happier circumstances, mes enfants.'

Monsieur says nothing as he drives at breakneck

speed along the dark roads. Becks and I must have dozed off, because it only seems like a few minutes before we're blinking at the bright lights of the airport. Monsieur pulls over, his face tense. 'The tickets will be at the Air France desk. You must make your way very quickly inside.'

'Are we late for the flight, Monsieur?'

He shakes his head. 'There is plenty of time. But you must be watchful for your own safety. Until Bertolini is taken, you will always be looking over your shoulder. Now go, my friends.'

We crawl sleepily out of the car, flexing stiff legs. Monsieur embraces each of us with strong arms, then gives us a gentle push in the back. 'Allez-y! And go safely.'

I grab Becks' hand as we stumble towards the entrance of Marseille Marignane airport. The air is warm, a soft breeze blowing in our faces. I take a last look back, and see the Merc disappearing into the grey dawn. And I remember that bright knife still lying beneath the driver's seat.

CHAPTER 5

Over The Gorge

'Have you got your passport, Becks?'

'No, I thought I'd chuck it in that bin over there.'

'Alright, just checking …'

'Sorry.'

'Your turn to stop saying sorry.'

We collect the tickets, and look around for somewhere to sit during the two hour wait. It's five in the morning. The departure lounge is almost empty. Two dudes with a week's growth of beard who look like students are crashed out on a row of seats. Behind them, a tired-looking woman tries to quieten a sobbing child. As we wander past, the little kid drops his dummy. I retrieve it, and hand it to his mum. Hesitantly, she takes it from me, her eyes wary.

Becks whispers, 'We must look like a teen version of Men in Black.'

'Looks like that cop thinks so, too.' Short and wiry, he's stood by the exit, a gun in his belt. He's got a face like his girlfriend's just told him he's too old for her. And he doesn't take his eyes off me. Is he wondering if I fit the description of the terrorist who trashed that cafe? I sit down quickly to look less tall.

I try to keep a look out for a black coat with a big head on top of it. But my eyes keep closing. And anyway, no one could wear a coat in this stuffy heat. I whisper vaguely to Becks, 'What do you think Bertolini wears under his coat?'

She stares at me. 'You don't want to know that.'

'No, I mean, what if …?'

Then I must have dozed off. Becks gives me a dig in the ribs as our flight's called.

—⁂—

The moment we're on the plane, my eyes snap shut again like hatches. I dream of hounds as huge as bullocks. They're baying after us as we stumble across rutted mud. Suddenly, we've got wings. We fly effortlessly through a dark, moonless sky. For some weird dream reason, Becks is wearing a nightdress, like Wendy in Peter Pan. And like Wendy, she just won't stop nagging. 'Down there, Joe. We have to land there!' Looking down, I see Monsieur's chateau, with three lonely lights burning. Then, Wendy's voice is right in my ear. 'Joe, do you want to get off this plane or not?'

Half-asleep, we stagger through the Heathrow Customs. I can't see any police. As she checks our passports, the woman gives us a friendly smile. 'You've grown up a bit since these photos were taken. On your way, now.'

We head out of the terminal, while Becks stuffs her passport back into her bag and mutters, 'I hate that photo of me with plaits!'

'I thought you looked cute with your chubby little cheeks.'

'Well, you looked like a toad.'

'I like toads.'

A blast of rain hits us as we join the queue on the station platform.

'Yuk! I prefer French rain. It's not as cold as this.' Becks takes a hair brush out of her bag and tries to drag it through matted red curls.

I run a hand through my own hair and find an insect that I've never seen before. Looks like a cross between a tiny wood louse and a millipede. I put it carefully on the ground. It's all curled up but maybe it'll uncurl and go on its way. 'We'll go back and live in Aix one day, Becks. I'll get a job, polishing the fountains, and you can teach English at the Uni. I can just see you with a prof hat on.'

She gives up on the hair thing, and stuffs the brush slowly back into her bag. Her voice is so tired. 'When is this 'one day', Joe? When can we go home?'

'When Monsieur has got his son back and Bertolini's been arrested. Now let's get to Monsieur's place. Then we can make a plan.'

'To get Arnaud back to his dad? How are we ever going to do that?'

'We just are, that's all.'

'Maybe we should talk to DI Wellington? I mean, he's got the memory stick with all that stuff from Monsieur's computer.'

'That would blow Monsieur's cover completely. I just wish we'd had time to take a copy.'

'Or never handed it over?'

44

'Sometimes I think that too.'

'And Joe ... we never had a chance to ask ...'

I put my arm around her shivering shoulders. 'Monsieur said that he worked with Dad once, then everything changed. Maybe what changed was losing his son to Bertolini.'

'And then it could have looked as though Monsieur had turned, letting his business be used as a drug running cover? I mean ... it looked like that to you at first, didn't it?'

'So unless he knew or guessed at the truth, Dad would have seen Monsieur as a traitor ... an enemy.'

Becks frowns. 'Suppose he still does?'

—⁓—

The train finally arrives. We pile into a carriage where every seat is taken, and stand squashed together, shoulder to shoulder with an army of commuters. Most of them are on their mobiles, shouting at the tops of their voices into a plastic stick jammed into their ears.

Then my mobile goes. 'Oh God, it's bound to be Mum. I wish I'd turned it off.'

But I've never heard this woman's voice before. It's high-pitched and bossy, like my Maths teacher. 'Joe? Am I speaking to Joe?'

I remember Detective Inspector Wellington's warning. 'If someone you don't know tries to contact you ...' The train stops, and most of the travellers in our carriage form a jostling queue for the door.

'Who are you?'

Becks is watching intently.

'My name is Charlotte Wickham, Joe. I'm a journalist working for a national newspaper. Is it convenient to talk?'

'Not really.' I wish I could plug Becks into this. Her eyebrows are joined up, like she's wondering if it's police. Perhaps it is police, fishing for information on Monsieur. Or maybe it's another shadow on the wall.

'I've been in touch with Jamie Johnson, Joe. He's the brother of a mate of yours, isn't he?'

'He … I … I don't know …'

'Jamie was working for a company called L'Étoile Fine Wines when he was jailed for drug running. Did you work for them too, Joe?'

'I … why do you want to know?'

'Because I have some information about a man known as Alfredo Bertolini.'

I almost drop the phone. When I get it back up to my ear, the woman is still there. 'I said, do you recognise that name, Joe?'

I'm starting to feel annoyed at this inquisition. 'Give me one good reason why I should tell you.'

Charlotte Wickham gives a little laugh. 'Oh, I can give you plenty of good reasons, Joe. And they're all printed on the Queen's currency. We can talk about how many good reasons you want when we meet, can't we?'

I take the phone away from my ear and stare at it like it's got a contagious disease. Becks whispers, 'Who is it?'

I cover the mouthpiece. 'A journalist. She thinks I want money.'

'In return for what?'

'Telling her if I know Bertolini. She says she's got information on him.'

'Hello … hello … can you still hear me Joe?'

'Tell her to take a hike!'

'No, wait, Becks. She could have information we need, couldn't she? Something that could help us get Arnaud back to Monsieur?'

'She just wants her story, Joe. IF she's a journalist.'

'What have we got to lose? She wants a meeting.'

'You don't even know if she's who she says she is. She could be someone Bertolini's sent to trap you.'

'Are you still there, Joe …?'

'We've got to take a chance, Becks.'

'Great! Let's ignore everything DIW said.'

Becks glares at me as I put my terminally ill phone back to my ear. 'I'm still here. Where do you want to meet?'

—៷៷—

'Doesn't look Deeply Unfashionable. Just your usual Victorian terraced.' Becks pauses, hand on the wooden gate that opens onto a path around fifteen feet long, leading to the front door with its neat little porch. Everything's in miniature, compared with Monsieur's huge chateau.

I struggle to hang onto the overflowing Sainsbury's carrier bags. 'It's a good distance from where Arnaud plays with his cutlery collection when he's in Bristol, and that's fine by me.'

'Did we remember to buy milk?'

'Yes! Now let's get inside. We must look like burglars casing the joint.' I look around as I put the key in the door, but I can't see anyone except an old lady outside the house opposite. She's clipping her hedge; wearing overalls, gardening gloves, wellies, a headscarf and goggles. Perhaps she's off on a mission to Afghanistan, once she's conquered the privet.

I close the door behind us. A tiled floor in the narrow hallway leads to the kitchen, with a sitting room on the right. Carpeted stairs go up to the floor above.

In the kitchen, Becks grabs the bags off me, and takes out a lasagne ready meal. She opens the microwave. 'Everything looks brand new.' Cupboard doors open and close, drawers are pulled out and there are exclamations about spiders as Becks explores her new kingdom.

I wander into the sitting room, and sit down on the sofa. On the walls are pictures of Provence; fields full of lavender, with deep blue skies above full of darting swallows. A photo of Aix shows the Cours Mirabeau with its shady cafes, tall plane trees and gushing fountains. I can almost hear the sparkling water. How I wish I was back there now with Becks. And that we'd left that cafe just sixty seconds earlier.

She comes in and bounces onto the sofa. 'No TV! How are you going to cope without Top Gear?'

'No time to watch it anyway. Not if we're going to get to the Downs by …'

BANG!

We fly over the back of the sofa and crouch on the floor.

Becks whispers, 'It came from the kitchen.'

'Keep down!'

We wait for the footsteps. Nothing. Bertolini must be lighter on his feet than he looks. There's just the humming of the microwave. I glance up, expecting to see those hard dark eyes right above us. 'Which way for a quick exit?'

'The windows have locks. Don't think we could do a stunt dive without ending up in A and E.'

I'm about to whisper, 'Beats the mortuary!', when the microwave goes Beep, beep, beeep!, and there's another bang but just a muffled one this time.

I peer cautiously round the sofa, and sniff. A strong smell is wafting out of the kitchen. It isn't gun smoke. 'Did you read the instructions, Becks?'

'Course I did. It said eight minutes.'

'And the bit about piercing the lid?'

While Becks cleans exploded lasagne off Monsieur's microwave, I grab a loaf and a pack of bacon from the carrier bag and stick some rashers under the grill. 'Bacon sarnies coming up.'

'Keep an eye on it, then. You set our grill on fire last time you cooked bacon.'

'That IS rich …! Coffee?'

'I'll make it. You watch the bacon.'

My mouth is full of bread and bacon as we sit on the sofa. Becks says quietly, 'These must be Arnaud's clothes we're in, mustn't they?'

I look at our black jeans and shirts. They're completely different sizes, or her jeans would be way too big. I swallow and nod.

'When Madame was going through the drawers

upstairs, I could see they were full of boys' clothes. Must've gone back a long time. And all of them were black. Arnaud wore nothing but black for years.'

'I've never seen Monsieur in anything but black, either.' A sudden squall blasts rain against the sitting room windows. I glance at my watch. 'It's time we got going.'

The front door closes behind us with a quiet click. Drizzle is soaking us again, when Becks whispers, 'Did you hear that?'

'Yep, I definitely heard the door close.'

'Not that! I thought I heard something inside, just before …'

'What kind of something?'

'Like … I don't know … a soft thud on the stairs?'

'Shall we go back and take a look?'

'Yes … no! We'll miss the bus.' She heads for the gate. 'These old houses must be full of creaking floorboards.'

I raise my hands over my head and flap them at her. 'And ghooosts!'

She shrieks with laughter as we race for the Clifton double-decker that's coming slowly down the hill. Five minutes later, we're looking down at the docks from the top deck. Below us is the building site where the wreck of Monsieur's office block sent a huge column of black smoke into the sky, the morning after the explosions that tore it apart. Scaffolding's everywhere now, and tall cranes are busy lifting giant girders into place. A few more months, and it'll be like that blue glass palace never existed.

The bus turns away from the docks, and starts to

groan up Park Street, towards the Gorge. Rain is running down the windows.

'Arnaud's house isn't far from the Observatory, is it?'

'About a quarter of a mile.'

'So, why did you agree to meet this journalist there? If that's what she is.'

'Her idea. Something about 'blending in with the tourists'. Like, you don't get spotted in a crowd.'

'Like you didn't get spotted in Aix in a crowd?'

'Bertolini and Arnaud are probably still in France, Becks. Monsieur got us onto the first flight out of Marignane this morning.'

'I still think a nuclear bunker would be a better venue than the Observatory. And what exactly is she offering you?'

'Oh, nothing much. Maybe just some stuff that could help us get Bertolini locked up for good, the police off Monsieur's back and his son home again. Knowledge is power, Becks.'

'In return for that tired cliché, here's another. There's no such thing as a free lunch. Especially not from a newspaper reporter!'

'She's not buying us ... Oww!'

The Observatory's a kind of Tardis. From the outside it looks like this small tower, near the suspension bridge. But the narrow, spiral steps inside just go on and on, till you feel like you'll end up in the clouds.

Becks wrinkles her nose. 'Smells stale.'

People push past us going down while we're trying to go up. At last we're at the top, in the middle of a crowd waiting to go in. I look round, trying to make out faces in this shadowy place. The crowd starts to move, and we're carried along into the Camera Obscura. The room is lit only by the slowly changing image of the Downs and the suspension bridge, reflected into a shallow bowl like a huge bird bath, by the rotating mirror at the top of the tower.

Becks stares at the image. 'Why's it black and white?'

'I don't know. It's weird, isn't it? Like you're looking into the past.' We watch the cars crawling across the bridge.

'Everything looks like it's in slow motion …. but it can't be.'

'We got Jack to go outside and try and get into the image, once. He told us he went running around all over the place, jumping up and down and waving his arms. But we never saw him.'

'That's creepy.'

'It was funny, actually, although Jack didn't think …'

Someone taps me on the shoulder. I whip round and back off, bumping into Becks.

'It's Joe, isn't it?'

The woman behind us is in a trouser suit, and her hair has highlights that are so bright, I can even make them out in here. I retort, 'It's Miss Wickham, isn't it?'

'Charlotte, please. Good to meet you at last, Joe. Here, my card.'

'This is Becks.'

'I wasn't expecting you to bring a friend.'

'I wasn't expecting you to contact me, Miss Wickham. Now, can we get on with this, please?'

'Yes, of course. Thanks for coming up here, I just thought …'

Then we're all three pushed apart by more people crowding inside. The room has gone quiet. Everyone's just gazing into this huge dish with its silent black, white and grey picture show. And I'm staring at a tiny figure, walking up from the edge of the Gorge towards us. It's stopped raining and the sun's coming out, but I still can't see very clearly. It looks like a young guy, shoulder length dark hair blowing behind him. He's keeping away from the groups of tourists wandering around. And still walking towards the Observatory.

I look quickly around the dark room, and elbow my way through the crowd to Becks. 'I thought I saw Arnaud. Coming up here.'

'What – in the image? Where?'

I look back into the dish. 'He's gone. He must be out of range of the mirror now.'

'He can't be here, Joe. Now let's find this woman, hear what she has to say and get out. Look, she's over there.'

'We can't talk in here.'

'So we find somewhere else!'

We move across to the journalist. She's watching those images too. I wonder if she's seen what I thought I did. She jumps as I say, 'There's a place down below where it's a bit quieter.'

She follows as we take the steps three at a time, stopping to wait for her at the bottom, next to a sign for Outlook Platform. Then we go down more stairs, meeting no one on the way, and enter a cave with a view. The journalist's hesitating steps tap after us. From a railed platform, Becks and I look down on the river Avon, hundreds of feet below. Just across to the left is the ledge where we crawled out of that hole into the light.

Becks' hair blows round her face in the wind from the Gorge. She swipes it away. 'Just get her story, Joe. Don't let her use you for hers!'

I turn as Miss Wickham catches up, out of breath. 'Look, I really don't want to be here, you know? So please be quick.'

'I'll be as brief as possible, Joe.' She whips out a notepad and pen. 'Firstly, can you confirm that you know a young man called Lenny Johnson, and you're aware that his brother Jamie was jailed for drug running?'

'I haven't come here to answer questions, Miss Wickham. You said you had information.'

'I'll take that as a Yes. When Jamie went to court, I was covering the case. My paper had been informed by an anonymous source that Jamie was working for a drugs gang, a big one. He denied in court that he was working for anyone. But I didn't believe it. He looked scared, as though he was under pressure to take the rap himself. I visited him in prison; told him that my paper would campaign for his release, if he let me know who he was carrying those drugs for.'

'Your paper really would have done that?'

Ms Wickham's highlights blow around in another blast from the Gorge, as she gives Becks a look. 'We're well known for taking the part of the little man. Giving the underdog a voice.'

'What if the underdog just wants to lie low and not attract any more attention?'

Miss Wickham ignores Becks. 'Jamie wouldn't open up on the first couple of visits. But the third time I saw him, about six months from the end of his jail term, he asked me if I had heard of someone called Alfredo Bertolini.' She looks at me like she's expecting me to react, but I just look back at her, though my heart is starting to thump and my mouth feels dry.

Becks says, 'This place will be closing soon.'

'My editor got really excited. Said he had an undercover reporter on Bertolini's case already. Apparently, he's a Corsican billionaire. Suspected of running a massive drugs operation on the European mainland. But this was the first hint of a link with the UK.'

Becks must be proud of how stone-faced I'm looking. The journalist's business-like voice starts to sound irritated. 'Does none of this mean anything to you, Joe?'

Becks says, 'You've got five minutes.'

'I last visited Jamie a few days before his release. I had to wait, because there was someone else talking to him. He had his back to me, but I could see he was a big, bulky man, with black hair. As he left, I got a look at his face. He had swarthy skin and dark eyes, with thick eyebrows. He looked at me really hard as he walked past. A very direct stare. You could call it pretty rude, in fact.'

She looks at me again to see if I recognise her description. I don't say anything, but my pulse is racing now. Becks glances pointedly at her watch, then back at Miss Wickham.

'Jamie was in total non-transmit. Whatever his visitor had said to him, he hadn't told him to have a cosy chat with me. I gave up, wished him well on his release and left. But I did talk to someone that afternoon and this is where you come into it, Joe.'

The tannoy announces that the Observatory will be closing in one minute.

'As I got back to my car, Jamie's visitor was waiting for me, leaning casually on the driver's door, smoking a small cigar. Without any preamble, he asked me why I'd been in to see Jamie. I was tempted to tell him to get lost, but I was interested as well. I gave him the same story that I'd told Jamie. He just smiled contemptuously. Then he said, 'You've been talking to the wrong person. If you want your story, ask Jamie's brother. Ask Lenny who his friend Joe was working for when the office block in the docks went up.' Then he stubbed out his cigar on my door mirror and walked off.'

The tannoy shouts that it's closing time. Miss Wickham's eyes are fixed on mine. This time, she gets a reaction. But not from me.

'Have you told the police?'

The journalist looks like she wishes Becks would disappear through a trap door in a cloud of smoke. 'I wanted Joe's side of things first, of course.'

'For your story? Is that it?'

'It's a matter of public interest if a drugs gang framed Jamie for a racket that he has nothing to do with.'

'It's a matter of police interest first and you know that. Sorry Miss Wickham, you've got a habit of talking to the wrong person, haven't you?'

Becks and I are heading for the stone stairway when the journalist says, 'He called me yesterday, Joe. Jamie's visitor.'

We keep going. She shouts after me, 'He said to tell you, 'The son goes home if the driver comes back'. Do you know what he meant?'

The stairs go dark. The lights are being switched off. We race up the steps. The security guard glares at us, as he lets us out into the late afternoon sun on the Clifton downs. It doesn't feel warm enough to be summer.

—⁂—

'What did he mean? Some kind of horrible deal?'

As the room grows darker in Monsieur's Bristol house, I sit with Becks on the sofa, staring at the images of Provence on the walls. They so remind me of the pictures in Monsieur's cave room, just before everything started to go up.

'You can't go back to Bertolini, Joe.'

'Going back might be the only way forward.'

'He's tried to kill you, four times! How many more do you want?'

'That was then. Before his Bristol shop went up in smoke.'

'So now his trigger finger must be really twitchy.'

'He knows who lit the fuse. I'm not his main target, Becks.'

'Can't we tell DI Wellington about all this? Get his big guns on the case?'

'Think about it, Becks. Bertolini still has Arnaud.'

'The police must be getting closer now.'

'Does it look like it? Five whole months after we handed that memory stick to DIW, Bertolini's still playing with shooters.'

'Do you think Monsieur has done a deal with Bertolini? Trading you for Arnaud? He'd never do that … would he?'

'I think, when you're a parent, you'd do anything to get your kid out of trouble.'

'But Arnaud hates his dad. And he's crippled with cocaine. He threw a knife at Monsieur! Why would he want to go back to him now?'

I'm trying to get into Arnaud's head. It hurts, because I've been there briefly before. 'He just might have changed his mind. Realised who Bertolini is … what he does to people …'

'Or … maybe he's no more use to Bertolini as a hostage. Now that Monsieur's blown everything up.'

'Doesn't explain why they'd send him home. Bertolini would more likely kill Arnaud and make sure that Monsieur knew about it.'

Becks gets up, and flicks the light switch. The wall lamps come on in a soft glow, like that room full of shadows in Monsieur's chateau. She turns to me. 'So the message must be some kind of trick.'

I reach into my back pocket for Miss Wickham's card. 'There's only one way to find out.'

'Can't you at least talk to Monsieur first? Ask him what on earth's going on?'

'I don't know if I want to ask him, Becks.'

The journalist's unsurprised voice tells me she

was expecting my call. 'Yes, Joe, I'm sure I can fix up a meeting with Jamie's visitor.' Then her voice hardens. 'But you have to brief me on the background. This story is going to be the biggest I've ever run. What's the deal all about, Joe?'

'I don't know any more than you about any deal. That's why I have to talk to this guy. You can be there if he's OK with it and you want to risk it. But it has to be in a public place, where people can see us.'

She pauses. 'He's OK with it because he knows I'm his only hope of getting to speak to you. So at least give me something to go on, Joe. Are you the driver who's going to be exchanged for the son? And who is this son? Whose son is he? '

'I was one of their drivers. I worked for Bertolini.' I hear her breathe in sharply, as I hand her this piece of information that I can easily afford to part with. 'Now, are you going to fix up this meeting?'

'I'll call you back tonight.'

Becks watches me, twisting a strand of red hair round and round her index finger. Then she jumps up and goes into the kitchen. 'Chef's special tonight is bacon sarnies à la Bristol, or Coco Rocks.'

'Mustn't get into a rut. Let's Rock, Becks.'

The journo calls back two hours later. 'Jamie's visitor will see us tomorrow morning at eleven, Joe.'

'Venue?'

'Saint Mary Redcliffe. I take it you know the place?'

'I know it.'

Becks looks up sleepily, head buried in the sofa cushions. 'Is it on?'

59

'It's on.'

As she snuggles back into the sofa, I get up quietly and go into the kitchen to make myself a coffee. Wondering if I'm getting another message from Jamie's visitor, in a code that's even harder to read than the first. Saint Mary Redcliffe Church overlooks the docks, where L'Étoile Fine Wines' offices went up in blue glass fireworks five months ago.

CHAPTER 6

The Slave Trader

'It's way more beautiful than the cathedral.' Becks gazes up at the tall, graceful spire of this huge church as we walk slowly towards it. On our right is the building site where the new office block will soon be rising into the skies.

'I used to stare out from my posh apartment and wonder if it had a massive organ that played as loud as they do at gigs. I was really missing going to gigs.'

'Does it?'

'No idea. I hardly went anywhere when I wasn't driving fine wines and cocaine all over the place. Never knew when I'd get the next shout.'

'Listen!'

Long, slowly changing chords are drifting through the still morning air. The deep, rumbling bass makes my spine tingle.

The journo is standing outside the entrance, making notes. Like this towering old church with its soul searching music has started her thinking about what she's going to write in her newspaper when she makes the front page. She frowns when she sees Becks. Tough.

'He told me he'd be inside.'

We walk behind her through the tall wooden door. It's cool and dark inside Saint Mary Redcliffe. Soft rainbow beams of light shimmer through the stained glass windows. Some tourists are walking quietly around, looking at their leaflets and gazing up at an arched ceiling so high, it makes my neck ache.

There's a young couple sitting in one of the pews at the back, talking in low voices. Perhaps they're planning to get married here. Right at the front, in view of the altar and two arched windows, one above the other, that blaze coloured light, is a man in a dark coat. All I can see are his broad shoulders and the back of his head, with its thick black hair. My heart thuds as I keep on walking with Becks. She flicks me a glance; she's spotted him too.

Miss Wickham stops next to the pew, and waves me in to sit next to him. Then she shoves herself in front of Becks to sit beside me. He turns, and even in the shadows I know it isn't Bertolini. But I can see, from the slow, satisfied smile on his face, that this dude knows me.

Now, it's as though it's just him and me sat there. I can hear the journo fumbling around in her bag for something but she might as well not exist. He's not looking at her. He says in a hoarse voice with a heavy accent, sounds Italian, 'You think you were brave to come here, Joe? Or just a fool?'

'You sent a message to me. I want to know what you meant.'

He asks another question without answering mine. I haven't answered his, so we're even. 'You remember me,

62

Joe? You should. I have been very close to you, on more than one occasion.'

I try to refocus on what I need to say to him, but part of my brain is on Call Divert, struggling to think back. 'I've never seen you before. Just stop wasting my time and tell me what you want.'

'You never saw me Joe, because I wasn't the one holding the gun.'

Although I now know I'm talking to Bertolini's driver, I'm a few months older and smarter now. And I've had it with this dude trying to freak me out. 'Then you'd better take some driving lessons. Or get a boss who can shoot.'

The smug smile disappears. I continue, 'This isn't a place for playing stupid mind games. If you don't want to tell me what that message was about, I'm gone. Thirty seconds. Clock's running.' I glance at my watch, and back at Driver.

He looks away from me, towards the altar. 'Arnaud is becoming ... difficult. We have found out that he is planning to return to his father. Alfredo sees him as a liability now. He could lead the police to us. Alfredo wants rid of Arnaud. But only if there is a deal.'

'Arnaud goes home if I come back? When I can lead the police to you too?'

Driver looks straight at me now. 'It is because of your police connections that Alfredo sees you as a possible asset. You know a lot about what they are doing. You also know how we operate. You could be very useful to us while we rebuild our network. We are offering you a deal. Five hundred thousand pounds for your co-operation. A year, at most. But your commitment must be total. Any sign that it is not, you will understand what it feels like to have a bullet in your head. Alfredo does not miss by accident. He enjoys a long chase.' Driver pauses. 'So do I.'

He knows this isn't a big enough threat. I've had four bullets close to my head already. 'Your Monsieur will also never see his son again. Except in a wooden box.'

'Why should I believe that Arnaud wants to be back with his father?'

'Why should you believe that it was Arnaud who threw the knife?'

I'm so still after he speaks, that for the first time I'm aware of Miss Wickham, sat in silence beside me. Her nervous fingers clutch her mobile, trying to position it where it can't be seen; she's recording this conversation. Driver must be that bit too far away from her to notice what she's doing.

I stare ahead at the vivid colours of the stained glass window, and an angel with shoulder length blond hair smiles benevolently back. Whatever I do now, whether I refuse or accept this deal, Monsieur is going to be punished again. If I tell Driver to get lost, they'll take another shot at me and this time they'll probably hit the bullseye, without that bullet-proof glass.

If I go over to Bertolini, Monsieur gets his son back, maybe. But what kind of son is going to return to him? Someone he can never trust or love again? As I weigh up the alternatives, I know I don't have a choice. But, considering what Commander Julius Grayling would do, perhaps I have an opportunity.

Driver's glancing at his watch now in a mocking imitation of me. 'Clock's running, Joe.'

I look straight at those hard, dark eyes. 'Eight hundred thousand. Twenty five percent up front, cash.'

His voice has a trace of respect. 'Tomorrow. I will call you about where we meet for the handover.'

He glances across at the journalist and suddenly I'm horrified that he knows what she's doing. He takes in Becks as she sits staring straight in front of her, and I go really cold now. But he just looks hard at me and says, 'No company, next time.' His heavy shape slips out of the pew almost silently, and he's gone.

The service is beginning. The priest and altar servers, their leader holding the cross high, walk in slow procession towards those huge windows that blaze vivid light. The organ's playing a hymn I know, from when I used to be an altar server: 'Oh God, our help in ages past, Our hope in years to come.'

We slide out of the pew and make our way quietly outside. The massive chords of the organ are still thundering in my ears as I take deep breaths of Bristol air. Becks slips her hand into mine. The journo grabs my arm. 'What were you saying in there, Joe? You couldn't have meant it – that you're going back to work for Bertolini?'

I shake her off, hanging on to Becks' hand like a lifeline. 'You brought me here, after your friendly little chats with Jamie. But you have no idea what this is really all about, do you?' She's silent, and I almost shout, 'DO you?'

She looks stunned at my anger. 'I was hoping … you would tell me.'

'Look, I'm sorry, Miss Wickham. But it's better for you that you don't know. These people are seriously dangerous. They don't care what they do.'

'Then why are you going back to them? You must be insane to get mixed up with them again.'

'I'm going back because I don't have any choice. And because I just might be able to do something to stop them.'

'What are you going to do with the recording, Miss Wickham?'

So Becks noticed, too. I squeeze her hand, and her fingers tighten around mine.

'I was going to take it to my editor. Now, I'm not sure …' She pauses. 'What do you want me to do with it, Joe?'

I lean against the solid stone walls of Saint Mary Redcliffe, looking up at the seagulls floating around overhead. My eyes wander to the water, where the ferry is quietly chugging towards Bristol Bridge. I feel so tired. I wish this journalist would just leave the whole thing alone, in case she gets caught up in it too and something horrible happens to her.

Becks says calmly, 'You have to take your phone to Detective Inspector Wellington, in Bristol Main Police Station, right now. Tell him everything you know.' Journo stares at Becks and gets a blast of brilliant green eyes in return. 'Get going, Miss Wickham. For the underdog!'

Miss Wickham looks hesitatingly at me. Then without a word, she turns and slowly walks away towards the city centre. We watch her as she disappears.

'Do you think she will go to DIW?'

'She'll go. She's scared.' Becks turns to me. 'What d'you want to do now?'

'While we wait for Driver's call? I don't know … something to take our minds off it? Bunjee jumping off the suspension bridge?'

'I would SO like to wash my hair, Joe!'

'That'll do.'

We take the bus back, and Becks dives into Sainsbury's. Half an hour later, I stagger out holding a carrier bag stuffed with enough shampoo, conditioner, shower gel, hair gel and soap to clean up a rugby team after a three hour head to head.

As we plod up the hill to Monsieur's place, my Special Forces old lady is outside her house again, still in full battle kit minus the goggles. This time she's kneeling on a cushion beside the grass verge, snipping the blades with scissors and sweeping the clippings carefully into a dustpan.

She looks up and I venture a smile. She smiles back, bright blue eyes twinkling beneath the headscarf. 'Y'aah right, lad? Mustn't let it get on top of you, must you?'

I'm mystified. Does she mean the bulging bag, Bertolini, or Life In General? 'No, 'course not.' Then I realise. 'You're winning, then?'

'Ooh, aah'll get these boogers, never fear!' She goes back to her snipping like she's beheading orcs.

'Joe! Shampoo!'

'Shampoo has landed.' I follow Becks up the path, and unlock the door. She grabs the bag and races up the stairs. As I turn to push the door shut, an arm grips my throat like a vice and a cold blade punctures my skin.

Like a reflex action I snap Arnaud's hold, dive forwards and roll. He makes another lunge at me. I twist sideways as the knife thuds into the floor beside my head, and vault to my feet. 'Touch it, and I'll break your neck!'

He stands there, breathing heavily. Sweat runs down his face. His hands shake, as though they're looking for the knife. Then he throws himself forwards and head butts me in the chest like a charging bull. Caught off balance, I stagger back into the kitchen. He lunges after me, picks up a chair and shoves it into my ribs, knocking all the air out of my lungs.

Gasping to get my breath back, I put the table between us. He chucks the chair at my head. I duck as it crashes into the window, glass flying everywhere. He picks up one of the jagged pieces and starts to move round the table towards me. Out of the corner of my eye, I see Becks frozen in the doorway.

I grab the table and pin him against the sink. He throws the piece of glass at my head. My ear stings as it flies past and smashes against the wall. Now, Arnaud's got no weapons left. And there's something very wrong with him. His legs give way. I let the table drop, as he slides down the sink to the floor. He takes quick shallow breaths, while his whole body trembles. I wheeze, still trying to get some air back, 'Can we talk?'

He slowly moves his head, his face grey. Becks and I help him into a chair in the sitting room. His head rolls back and he closes his eyes.

She whispers, 'I'll do coffee. You keep an eye …'

She pulls the knife out of the hall floor, chucks it through the hole that was the kitchen window, then goes to switch on the kettle.

I grab a tea towel, knot it round my neck to stop the warm trickling stuff then go back into the sitting room. Arnaud is lying very still in the chair. I can just hear these small panting breaths that barely move his chest. I'm feeling scared for him now. Wondering if I should call an ambulance I crouch down by the chair, watching him. 'Arnaud, can you hear me?'

Becks brings three mugs of black coffee, and puts one down on the small table beside him. He makes a huge effort to sit up. His hands are shaking so much that he can hardly grip the mug.

I sit down slowly in the chair opposite Arnaud and stare at Monsieur from years ago. Long black hair instead of short-cropped silver. Same chiselled cheekbones. Intense eyes, dark, not the grey of Monsieur's, that look at me now with so much pain and fear. And I thought it was hate I saw that afternoon in Aix. I must have been feeling very scared myself to think that.

'Why did you come here, Arnaud?'

He takes another of those quick breaths and says slowly, his English as perfect as his father's, 'I had to get away from him.'

'Bertolini?'

With an effort, he nods. Another quick breath. 'I was trying to get clean. Slowly, one day at a time.' He swallows. 'I wanted to be free of them.' He wipes the sweat off his face with his sleeve.

I'm thinking more clearly now as my lungs fill up

again. 'Free of the drugs? Because that's the only way you can get free of Bertolini?'

Another slow nod. I can see how difficult it is for him to talk and I'm beginning to realise why. 'Then they saw what you were trying to do? So they took it all away from you – the drugs, the money to buy them?'

He looks at me through a haze of pain. 'How did you know?'

'I know what gives Bertolini his fix. He enjoyed getting you onto them, didn't he? Now he's enjoying watching you trying to get off them. Even if it kills you.'

He takes a sip of the coffee, shivers and puts the mug down unsteadily. I'm still trying to piece Arnaud's story together for him; he looks too ill to talk much. 'You came here to hide. They don't know about this place. When I turned up you thought you could be wrong. Did you think they'd sent me?'

He stares at me as though he's trying to see right into my brain and whispers, 'Are you saying they didn't send you?'

'That's what I'm saying.'

And I think, if Driver hands over all that money tomorrow and I belong to Bertolini again, I could be the one they send after Arnaud. But it isn't tomorrow, yet.

I decide that Arnaud must be telling the truth. No one could fake looking so ill, so at the end of everything. 'Your father gave us the keys to this house, Arnaud. Bertolini's after us, too.'

'My father …?'

'They want him, most of all. I don't know what

version Bertolini's given you but it was your dad who blew up the Bristol office.'

His dark eyes widen in surprise again. 'He said … a rival cartel …'

'Bertolini wouldn't want you to know the truth, would he?' I look at his exhausted face. 'Your dad told us that he's always wanted you back with him.'

'My father wants me to return?' I see a light in his eyes that wasn't there before.

'How can we help you, Arnaud? Where do you want to go?'

His eyes close as his head rolls back onto the chair again, and I think he's going to pass out. He says, so quietly between his shallow breaths that I have to lean forward to hear him, so quietly that he could be talking in his sleep, 'Heimat.'

I have no idea what that word means. 'Arnaud, there isn't much time. Where do you want to go? You must tell us!'

He breathes out the last word. 'Home.'

Now I can hear another sound that's just as faint, but getting louder all the time. Becks has heard it too. We gently lever him up. 'Arnaud, we have to go, now.'

He murmurs a protest.

'There's a cop car on the way!'

We stumble out of the back door and into the garden. Becks says, 'Through the gate at the end. Come on!'

We half carry Arnaud through it, and start to struggle down through the back streets. A young woman with a push chair sees us and quickly crosses the road.

'Where are we going, Joe?'

'City centre. Then bus or train to Bristol Airport.' I yank the blood-stained tea towel off my neck and chuck it into a bin, just as three dudes sway out of a pub opposite. They stop dead in their tracks, and one of them starts to punch a number into his mobile. 'Keep moving!'

Nee Naw, Nee Naw! After that smashing glass, police cars must be heading for the house in Knowle West from all directions. As we hit the main road down to the city centre, I remember the envelope that Monsieur gave us, still tucked into my back pocket. I steer the three of us into a bus shelter. 'Pit stop.'

I rip open the envelope, and count. Monsieur has given us one thousand pounds in fifty pound notes, and another thousand in Euros. A couple of dudes in hoodies propped up against the wall nearby watch these three loaded hobos with interest.

I take out a handful of notes, stuff the envelope back into my pocket and stick my hand out for the next taxi. It drives straight past. The second slows down as the driver takes a look at us, then accelerates away. The third taxi stops and the driver gets out and walks over. He's about the same age as Grandad, but with more hair, a sandy fringe flopping over his face. He looks at Arnaud. 'You guys in some kind of trouble?'

Becks goes for an Oscar. 'We have to get our mate to Bristol Airport. He missed his flight to France to go back to his dad because he's not very well, and he's on this medication that makes him really tired and sleepy?'

I hold out some notes. 'We'll pay you up front. How much?'

'Just the usual twenty. Pay me when we get there.'

This driver isn't like the one we met in Saint Mary Redcliffe this morning. He has a kind face. He helps us to get Arnaud into his car.

In the taxi, Arnaud falls into a troubled sleep. His head turns from side to side, and he murmurs words in languages I don't understand. Sometimes his hands move restlessly, like they're trying to find something. I can guess what. I have no idea what it's like being on drugs or trying to come off them, but I can imagine the awful place he's in.

Becks looks worried. 'Call Monsieur, Joe!'

I try. 'No answer. Not even voicemail.'

The driver glances back at us. 'You guys OK?'

'We're OK, thanks.'

I wonder what could have happened to Monsieur since we last saw him at Marseille Marignane airport. After that drive with the air blasting through the rip in the convertible hood. The rip that we all thought Arnaud's knife had made.

As I offer the twenty pounds to the driver he says, 'Make it ten. I'll get a return fare from here, no problem.'

'That's really good of you.'

Arnaud holds out a hand that looks a bit steadier than it did half an hour ago. 'My thanks to you, sir. You are most kind.'

The taxi driver takes Arnaud's hand gently. 'You get back to your dad now and get well. Alright?'

Becks and I walk slowly with Arnaud into the airport. As I buy his ticket, I'm thinking about tomorrow. When I might have to become his hunter.

Becks rushes off. She comes back a few minutes

later with a sandwich pack and thrusts it into his hands. 'Make sure you eat them.' He nods, a familiar half-smile on his tired face.

His flight is called. I peel off another handful of notes and pass them to him. 'Go safely, Arnaud. Take care!'

'Goodbye … my friends.' He hugs us, weak as he is, and we hug him back. We watch his thin figure disappear through the departure gate.

'He's still so pale. I wish we could go with him.'

'So do I. But it might keep Bertolini away from him for just a bit longer if I show up for my fun rendezvous tomorrow.'

We're walking out of the airport when Becks says, 'We can't go back to the house. Police could be watching it.'

I look at my watch. It's half eight and getting dark. 'Ever dossed outdoors?'

'Once, for a bet with Steve. Never again!'

'Never say never again, Becks …'

We take a taxi back to Bristol and get out at the top of Park Street.

'There's a little square just up here with some benches. I found it once when I was shopping for clothes.'

'Benches.'

'Well, I didn't notice any bunk beds with duvets.'

'Or any power showers with shampoo?'

'Only seven more hours then the snack shops'll open.'

'Seven hours! I'll die of hypothermia!'

I look at Becks' pale face. 'Look, we could call Steve

– get him to pick you up. Bertolini's got other things on his mind now, with Arnaud on the run.'

'I'm not going home till you do! And we'll always be bad news for our families while that scum is on the loose.'

'OK. Let's find a five star bench.'

The street lamps cast more shadow than light over the little park with its trees and bushes, in the middle of a square of Victorian houses. 'That one, look, under the tree.'

Becks sits on it. 'Feels damp.'

'Just a bit of dew. Curl up and close your eyes, you'll soon be away.'

I try and take my own advice and find out after five minutes that man was not made to sleep on park benches. But I'm so tired that I must have dozed off. Then I hear Becks squeal, 'Get off me, you beast!' At the same time, a small something lands on my shoulder, and sharp claws dig into my neck.

In the shadows I see Becks leap up and whizz round, as she grabs at another small something and chucks it away from her. I yank at the furry animal that's shoving its nose into my ear and it jumps off into the tree.

'I forgot about the squirrels. People must feed them, they're so tame.'

'That one was as tame as Dracula!'

'They probably won't try it again, now they know we haven't got any food for them.'

'They'd better not.'

'Shhh!' A light's come on in one of the houses.

I've just got into another doze when the claws are in

our necks again. Becks mutters, 'I've HAD it with these flying rats.' She grabs her squirrel, then mine, by the scruff of their necks and I hear her feet swishing in the grass as she walks off purposefully towards Park Street. A few minutes later she's back, curling up her legs on the bench.

'What did you do with them?'

'Put them in a wheelie bin outside a Chinese. They'll be in their seventh heaven by now.'

'You didn't think to bring back any special fried rice?'

'Don't be disgusting.'

The flying rats don't come back, or if they do I'm too out of it to feel their claws. I dream about a huge boulder that's trying to push us off the ledge after we've climbed through the hole in the cliffs and ended up three hundred feet above the river. Every time it shoves me I try and shove back, but I keep getting pushed closer and closer to the edge. Then I go over into thin air, yelling.

My hands and knees bump into the grass of the park. The boulder has a black hairy coat and a gruff voice. It smells like a loo that hasn't been cleaned in a hundred years, but at least it isn't Bertolini. Becks is squeezed as tight as she can get into the corner of the bench.

'GerrOUT! MINE!' He has an encampment of carrier bags around him, bulging with old clothes and bottles. In the dim light of the street lamps, I try to make out his face through the straggly grey beard and rat tails of hair trailing from his bald head. Now he's shoving himself towards Becks. She slides off the bench to get out of his way.

I whisper, 'Sorry … we didn't know it was yours … have a good night.'

He grunts, and starts to take a bottle out of one of the bags, as we tiptoe towards the opposite side of the park.

'Why didn't you tell me this is THE place to hang out in Bristol? I'd have brought my party dress.'

'Quiet – there's a door opening over there.'

The woman silhouetted in the doorway seems to be wearing a dressing gown, and she's shining a torch into the park. We flatten ourselves in the grass.

'Henry? Henry! It's them again. Call the police!' No one replies from inside the house, and Greybeard doesn't seem too bothered. We hear a long, rumbling belch, then the scrape of a bottle being unscrewed. The torch beam is feeble as it wanders around the shadowy park.

'P'raps she lives on her own and this is like the nightly routine? Poor old thing.' Becks suppresses a sneeze. 'Why am I feeling sorry for her? I'm catching pneumonia here!'

After a few more Henries the door closes. We stagger across to a bench as far away as possible from Greybeard the Master Belcher. We must both have dozed off again when I hear giggles that seem to come from right behind us.

'How did you get the vodka?' It's a girl's voice.

'Big Bro.' More giggles. I hear Becks move slightly and I know she's awake too, listening.

'And did Big Bro bring the rest?'

Those last two words sting me like a whip. I grab Becks' hand without saying anything. As we slip under the railings, a police minibus pulls up quietly on the other side of the park. Dark figures silently pour out of it and head through the gate. We're back in Park Street when we see bright beams forking around the sky behind us, and a loud hailer goes, 'Police! Freeze!'

'What if they stop us?'

'We've been to a good party, and my dad's going to pick us up on College Green, OK?'

A squad car blasts up Park Street and slows down as it approaches. We keep walking. 'Try and look a bit happier, Becks. Like, it was a really great party?'

She puts on a grim smile. 'Unforgettable!'

The squad car drives on towards the park. We walk on down.

'Where are we going? I'm all partied out.'

'Temple Meads. The snack shops open there an hour earlier than they do in Park Street.'

When we make the station it's 5.00 am. Dawn is breaking over the city in thin strands of grey and pink cloud. We follow the smell of food into the cafeteria. Ten minutes later, we're stuffing down bacon and eggs. As we eat, I look around with the usual twitch of wondering if we're being watched. The cafe's busy, but it's mainly people in city suits with their brief cases, and tired tourists with backpacks.

Becks drains her hot choc and yawns. 'D'you think they'd notice if we went to sleep in here? It's so nice and warm, and they don't do small furry animals with claws.'

'I think they'd notice.'

We collapse onto a bench outside near the taxi rank.

We must both have slept like the dead and no one tries to move us on this time. I dream of being in my bed, Fats curled up beside me on my pillow, purring loudly in my ear. When I wake up, my head is on some dude's shoulder. He's snoring like a Pit Bull warming up for the kill. Becks is curled up next to me. I look at my watch. It's 10.55 am, and the sun is shining brightly, straight into my eyes. I give her a gentle nudge. 'Hello from your speaking clock, Becks.'

Her voice is full of sleep. 'Has Driver called?'

'Not yet.'

'What if he doesn't?'

'Ask me when today is over.'

I think about Arnaud. Trying to get home, like we so want to; but with demons inside him as well as behind him. I grab my phone. This time, I get Monsieur's voicemail. 'I regret that I am not available. Leave a brief message only if it is urgent.'

'We've met Arnaud, Monsieur. He wants to come back to you. He said he was going to somewhere called Heimat. Then he said home. He's very ill. And Bertolini's on his back.'

Seconds later, my mobile rings. I hope it's Monsieur. But it's the same voice I listened to in St Mary Redcliffe. 'Five minutes. Temple Meads taxi rank.'

'I'll be there.'

Becks' eyes are wide open now. 'Where and when?'

'Right here. Five minutes.'

'Just time to get my hair fixed.'

'He said no company, remember? It's time you took the train home, Becks.'

79

'I'm coming with you. You always get into a horrible mess when I don't!'

I look at my watch. Four minutes to go. No sign of Driver. I stand up and walk forwards a few steps to try and see better. Tourists are wandering around, dragging huge suitcases on wheels or staggering under heavy backpacks. Parents with irritable children in tow are pushing their way through the crowd. Friends shout a welcome as they find each other. I turn back to Becks. She's not there.

A Mercedes taxi pulls up sharply, right next to me. I remember looking at the driver and thinking, You aren't the dude in the church. Then I'm grabbed from behind, and something cold goes right into my spine. As it all goes black I wonder why it doesn't hurt.

CHAPTER 7

Vertigo

There's a thundering in my head. I'm being chucked from side to side. I can see the main sail of Grandad's dinghy like a huge white wing above me. It shudders and snaps as a strong gust hits it. The little boat veers wildly. I'm lying in the bottom of the boat and I can't get up to grab the jib. It flaps crazily without me to hold it. Every now and then we mount a ten-foot wave, then dive down the other side. The boat tips right over like we're going to capsize. Then amazingly, it bobs back up. We're sailing in darkness. It's as black as the storm that hit when I was trying to get out of Bertolini's gunsights on the M5.

I wake with a dull ache in my spine. The roar of helicopter rotors is in my ears. I stir slightly in the seat I'm tied into. Becks is in the seat opposite, tied up too. Her eyes are closed. What have they done to her? Becks!

Dazed, I stare out of the window at a deep blue sky. The copter swings round. Now, I'm looking down at two islands in an even deeper blue sea, off a mainland. We're heading down towards the smaller island, nearest the mainland. Most of it is grey craggy mountains, with woods on the lower slopes. As we go down further, I can make out a few towns on the coastlines; small villages are scattered around inland. We're going down faster now, heading for the mountains in the centre of the island.

Driver is in the pilot's seat. A dude I've never seen before is sat beside me, holding a revolver. He has a pale face and a bald head to match. Next to Becks is Alfredo Bertolini, drug running boss man who puts bullets into people for fun. It makes my skin crawl to see him so close to her.

Slowly, Becks opens her eyes. A huge wave of relief washes over me. She sees me and I try to do a 'We'll sort it somehow' grin. This doesn't go down too well with Baldy. He waves his gun in my direction. I nod. Just shut up and do as you're told. For now, anyway.

The copter is dropping down more slowly, circling round the top of a mountain. Where on earth do we land in this place? As we get to around three hundred feet, I can make out a flat area that looks like it's been hacked out of the mountain top. We're still falling towards it. Then dust flies everywhere, there's a jolt, and we've touched down.

Bertolini pulls Becks after him as I scramble out of the copter with Baldy, hands tied behind me. It feels Mediterranean, with that blue sea and sky. But I have no idea where we are; my Geography is rubbish. I glance back and see Becks looking around her, blinking in the strong sunlight.

Baldy gives me a dig in the back with his shooter. We all walk to a round metal plate about five feet across, at the side of the helipad. He yanks my arm to get both my feet on it. Suddenly it gives way and we're going down.

We're in a lift shaft with dim lights. I can hear an engine throbbing. I think it's a generator, as there couldn't be power lines up here to this mountain wilderness. I can feel the gun pushing into my back. It's like a grown up version of the ghost train on a fairground ride. The smell of these dudes is worse, though. Stale sweat mixed with garlic beats candy floss and ice cream anytime. I hear Becks draw in her breath and hold it.

The lift hits ground with a bump and a door slides open. I'm expecting something gold-plated because I wonder if this is Bertolini's mansion in Corsica that Monsieur told us about. It's pretty cool. Polished wood floorboards, Eastern-style rugs, carved wood tables, a well loaded bar. But it's the view that's the most impressive part.

In this semi-circular room, the windows look out onto miles of grey mountain peaks and beyond them, that blue sea. Two eagles cruise lazily around, looking for lunch. This has to be the ultimate penthouse suite. The windows are heavily tinted and the generator seems to be powering an air-conditioning system; so in spite of the blazing late-afternoon sun, the room is cool and comfortable.

The sightseeing tour's over. Baldy shoves me into an upright chair and lashes me to the back of it. Bertolini pushes Becks into a chair opposite. His driver/pilot/gofer takes his coat, and pours him a drink from the bar. Well, now I know what the man I used to call Big Head wears under his coat. The pink shirt bulges with the weight of his gut, as he sits down in a large armchair. He pulls a cigar from its aluminium case, and sniffs it appreciatively. The gofer lights it for him. Creep.

The last time I heard Bertolini's voice, he was telling me to drive to Birmingham with a bootload of Class A. His voice sounds the same now. Like he's smoked too many cigars and never goes to the gym. 'You disappoint me, Joe.'

I do wooden. No kicks for you from this little chat, Alfredo.

'You know why you disappoint me, Joe?'

I stare out of the window, admiring the view. Baldy smacks me across the shoulders with the butt of his gun. I've had worse knocks playing footie at school. Becks must have sussed that I'm doing Wind Up Bertolini, because although she jumps at the blow, she says nothing.

Bertolini's like a stand-up comedian who just isn't being fed the lines he wants. He's scowling. Good. Go on Alfredo, lose it and look a complete prat. I'll enjoy that.

'You were both seen with Arnaud at Bristol Airport yesterday.'

I'm still so annoyingly silent. Baldy's gun hits my head this time. I can't remember much for a bit after that. Fireworks go off in my ears and I can't hear or see very well. But at least it's easy now not to say anything. Bertolini's voice is mixed up with others in my head. I can hear Arnaud's exhausted, 'Heimat …. Home', and the old lady from the SAS, 'Mustn't let it get on top of you, must you?'

'You know where Arnaud is going don't you, Joe? We had a deal. You will tell us where he is going.'

I mumble, 'No cash, no deal.'

Becks jumps up. 'I'll tell you where he's going! But you've got to stop this!'

'Becks – no!'

She looks at me furiously. 'He's not worth it, Joe!' I stare at her. So do Bertolini and crew. I really hope Becks remembers to send me an autographed photo when she makes Hollywood. 'Arnaud said he was going to take the train from Marseille to Paris. He has friends there. They're going to take him onwards from Paris to Switzerland.'

I hold my breath. If Bertolini decides she's lying, Becks is in far worse trouble than I am. His black eyes narrow to slits as he stares straight into hers. 'Where in Switzerland?'

'I'm trying to remember … he said it's a small village in the Alps called … right, OK, I think he said it was called Villars.'

Becks isn't like me – she's good at Geography. But I hope she's being A$\star$ good at it now. Because this place has got to exist or we won't for much longer. Bertolini takes a step towards her, his huge bulk just inches away. Becks doesn't move, green eyes returning fire.

'You better be telling the truth, Signorina.' He turns and barks at Baldy, 'Lock the door behind us!' He and Driver go out and their feet clatter down some stairs.

Baldy saunters over to the door and turns the key, leaving it in the lock. Then he goes to the bar and perches on a stool, looking at us with a lop-sided sneer. He's still got the gun, stuffed in his belt.

Becks and I are careful not to exchange glances. She says, 'Is it … OK … if I sit down?'

'Y'might as well. But don' move!'

'Thanks.' Becks sits, obediently motionless. A few

minutes pass in complete silence. Then she wipes an imaginary drop of sweat off her forehead with a hand that trembles slightly. 'C – could I have a glass of water?'

'Nah.' He jerks his head towards the bar. 'No one touches the boss's stuff.'

'Not even you? But you must be his top gun!' Becks looks respectfully at Baldy. 'Or is that … the other one, the copter pilot?'

'That loser? 'E couldn't 'it a dead sheep from three feet.' Baldy reaches over the bar for a bottle of brandy, fills up a tumbler and takes several large gulps.

Becks has a timid smile on her face that I have never seen before. 'I … er … bet you can shoot, yeah?'

Baldy grins. 'I'm legend, me!' His fingers touch the gun in his belt but thankfully it stays where it is. He drains the glass, refills it, takes another slug then leans confidentially towards Becks. 'Took ou' a bear th'other day.'

Becks' eyes widen. 'A BEAR? Awesome!'

'Yeah, 'uge, it was. Came righ' at me. Got it firshsshot, shtraight 'tween th'eyes.' He takes another large swig.

'I guess you have to be prepared for anything in your job?'

'S'fact. Y'never know wha's comin'.' Another gulp of brandy. ' … too many bad men aroun'.'

Becks' voice is softly admiring. 'Your boss must depend on you so much …'

'Oh, 'e nee's me awright.' He refills the glass. 'Las' week, Marseille, we get jumped by four've Tarantino's … or wzz't ten?' Half of the glassful disappears down his throat.

Becks' eyes are almost popping out of her head. 'What happened?'

'Wasted th'lot of 'em, didn' I?' He finishes the glass and sways slightly on the bar stool as he picks up the nearly empty bottle. I move my arms to get a feel of the rope tying me to the chair. It's not as tight as Baldy is. I start to inch my way loose, stopping each time his increasingly glazed eyes take me in.

The Baldy Fan Club has hit fever pitch. 'Weren't you scared, taking them all on like that?'

'Don' do scared, me. Y'can't, not in zzz job. KnowotImean?'

'That is so cool. I bet your boss really appreciates you?'

'Yeah … yeah … 'ppreshates … zzzzword …'

The stool keels slowly over. Baldy's eyes are closed before he hits the floor. I let the ropes drop. Becks quietly slides open the window. The low evening sun is casting its last beams over the range of mountain peaks, carving deep shadows into their craggy slopes. We can just make out bits of a winding road, far below.

She whispers, 'Looks way further down than the bottom of the Gorge.'

My heart hammers as I stare at the drop. 'It's time to find out. They'll be back any minute.'

Beneath the window is a small ledge, about two feet wide. It follows the line of the building to the left, then disappears.

'It's funny, but I've not got any keener on heights since the Gorge, Joe.'

'Me neither. But the only way out of this is down.'

We jump as feet thunder back up the stairs. The door handle shakes, then someone tries to unlock the door but they can't because Baldy's left the key in. Bertolini roars at the unconscious Baldy on the other side.

I scramble out of the window, trying not to look down. Becks follows. The sun's sunk down behind the mountains, and it's too dark to see the drop now. I feel my way along the ledge, hanging on to the window frames. Then they're gone, but the ledge is still there. My hands search the sheer rock for a grip. 'I can find a way up but not down.'

'Try harder!'

In the room, kicks thud at the door and I start to panic. I kneel, groping in the dark. Slide my right foot downwards and find somewhere to put it. Reach out my right hand to search for something to hold onto. Nothing but flat rock face. I grope around some more and find a handle. 'I've got a hold. Follow me …'

A gun shot goes off in the room. They must have blasted through the lock.

'Keep going if you don't want my foot on your head!'

I move my left foot, inches at a time. Move my right foot again and there's nowhere for it to go. In my mind I can see this huge drop that we're dangling over. I shut down the image and imagine I'm on the climbing wall in Gloucester. It doesn't help much; I get shaky when I'm on that too.

Suddenly a bright beam splits the dark up above. Then it trails around the rock face where we're hanging on in a rubbish imitation of Spider Man. There's a shot. The rock I'm about to grab explodes. I duck as splinters fly past my eyes and my foot slips. I slide, clawing at the cliff face before jolting to a stop as my feet hit a small ledge. A second bullet smashes into the cliff just above my head. My heart is thumping so hard I think it's going to smash my rib cage.

Then the idea comes to me. 'You there, Becks?'

'Just!'

'I don't think they want to shoot us.'

'Oh, silly me. They want to take us for a candle-lit dinner?'

'They could have hit us easily by now. They want us to panic and let go.'

'They could have said!'

'If we can get into that gully down there we'll be out of sight.'

'What gully?'

'Just follow!'

The torch rakes the rock face again. Slowly, I start to feel my way down towards the crevice. Becks' feet slide down after me and stones fall on my head. Then she bumps down beside me. We tuck ourselves into the gully, away from that beam of light. Another bullet whistles past.

'Scream, Becks. Like we're falling.'

I let out a yell. She screams so loud that I think my eardrums may have ruptured and we're going to start an avalanche. Her voice echoes round the mountains. Then, silence. After a wait that feels endless the beam goes off.

'Was that a good scream, or what?'

'Sorry? Can't hear you …'

'I said …'

'Forget it.'

We carry on down blindly in the dark for hours, straining for a grip, slipping and sliding on the rock face. The night is warm. I'm pouring with sweat, every muscle trembling with the effort. Then, I realise that I can see more clearly. 'Look up there, Becks.'

The cloud cover has gone. Millions of stars glitter like diamonds on black velvet, with no light from towns between them and us. Suddenly, a shower of sparkling shooting stars rains earthwards.

She catches her breath. 'That is so beautiful!'

'Hey, and I can see pine trees below us.' A few minutes later we're in the cover of the woods.

'Damn.' Becks scrambles back to her feet. 'These pine needles are so slippery.'

'Hang on to the trees.'

'It's so dark again I … whoooh …!' Her voice disappears into the forest.

'Becks?' My feet suddenly slip into nothingness. I throw my hands out for a branch and miss. Now I'm sliding after her, faster and faster. Needles scrape my face as I crash into trees and bounce off them. Then I land in a heap.

'Your foot is in my ear.'

'Sorry. You alright?'

She gets up, shaking pine needles out of her clothes. 'Apart from the tree that hitched a lift.'

'This must be the road we saw from Bertolini's holiday home.' The brilliant starlight illuminates the twisting road that goes on down the mountain. Then, so does the glow of headlamps. 'Get down!' We hit the ditch. A black Porsche Carrera cruises past at 20 mph then takes the Z-bend below. 'I have never seen a Porsche drive as slowly as that.'

We start to walk down the mountain, keeping an eye out for more headlamps. Another shower of meteors blazes overhead.

'Why did you think they wanted to scare us into falling, and not just shoot us?'

'They didn't take anything off me when I was out of it. I still have the dosh that Monsieur gave us, and my passport. Have you got yours?'

She stuffs a hand into her jeans pocket. 'Still there. So?'

'So, our bodies would have been easy to identify. Sweet revenge for Bertolini on our families and Monsieur, not to mention us. And no bullet holes. No evidence that could stick.'

'That is horrible!'

'That is the way they are, Becks.'

'Car!'

We dive for cover again. It's another black Porsche Carrera, coming up the mountain this time, even more slowly than the first. Or is it the same one?

'Get right down!' A torch blazes out of the car window. Not breathing, we lie motionless in the pine needles. For a moment, I think the Porsche going to stop. Then it moves on at a snail's pace. The headlamps disappear. We give it a good minute before rejoining the road.

'Either black Porsche Carreras are the car of choice

in this place, de-tuned to drive at 20 mph max with high strength torches part of the specification or …'

'We need to get a lift!'

We tramp downwards through the Z-bends, on full alert now.

'That village in Switzerland, Becks …'

'Is real. A mate of mine went skiing there with the school a few years back. Dad didn't have the dosh. I was so green with envy that I never forgot the name.'

'What mate was that then? Could he ski like Bond?'

'SHE came back with a broken leg. The idiot went off-piste.'

'Shouldn't ever drink and ski … Oww! That was my only good ankle. Any idea what island we're on?'

'I think I saw the French mainland as we came down. So this could be Corsica. But there's a sign coming up, saying where we've been.'

Vivario. Not a name either of us is ever going to forget.

We've been trudging on down the mountain for maybe an hour. The sky is still firing shooting stars over us, when we hear a massive diesel engine. A blaze of headlamps comes slowly down towards the hairpin behind us. We're on a straight stretch of road now, maybe three hundred yards before the next bend. The truck's in a low gear as it makes the steep descent.

'Fancy trying for that lift, Becks?'

'My brain says Bertolini could like trucks as well as Merc taxis and helicopters. My legs say Just Do It!'

The monster trundles round the corner. I stick

my thumb out, really hoping that I'm not going to be garrotted for this. Three racks of headlamps on mainbeam completely dazzle us. Massive horns blare. There's the explosion of airbrakes coming full on, then a long screaming of huge tyres. We're about to dive off the road when the beast stops, the window's wound down and we get a crash course A-Level in how to swear, Corsican-style.

—∞—

Climbing up into that cab is like scaling the side of my house. I yank myself inside after Becks and wrench the door shut. In the cabin, there's a strong smell of garlic, red wine, stale sweat and French cigarettes. The trucker chucks the butt of a Gauloise out the window. He's so huge in his battered vest and jeans, he must steer with his belly.

'Français?' His voice reminds me of Bertolini's throaty growl.

'Anglais, Monsieur.' Becks' voice is nervously polite. 'Mais nous parlons Français un tout petit peu.'

His double chin wobbles as he leans towards us. 'Qu'est-ce que vous faites ici? Touristes?'

'Oui.' She explains that we got lost, hiking with some mates, and fell off the mountain.

'Vous êtes fous, vous savez? Il y a tant d'hommes méchants ici!'

We both nod. We are mad. And there are so many bad men around. I stare out of the window at the dark forests of pine trees, wishing he'd get his truck going.

Any minute now, that Porsche is going to cruise past again.

His big gut strains against the wheel as he shifts into gear. The air brakes go off with a hiss like a geyser. The massive diesel engine rumbles and shakes, and we move on slowly down the mountain. My eyes are out on stalks as I take in the transmission. It's way more complicated than the Bentley; looks like 18 gears. Truckie glances across at me, then back at the steep road. 'Vous aimez conduire?'

Reeling from the blast of garlic and wine I blurt out, 'Oui, je l'aime bien, Monsieur.'

Becks flicks me a quick glance, like, Why on earth did you have to tell this guy that you love driving? Her hands move around quietly, looking for a seatbelt. I can't find mine either, and I'm not about to ask. Any stupid questions, he's going to chuck us out onto the roadside.

Becks flicks the driver a cautious glance. 'Vous allez au port, Monsieur?'

'Calvi, bien sur.' His big hands swing the wheel. I feel sorry for anyone who might be coming the other way, as we take the Z-bend on both sides of the road. All I can see is a sheer black drop right below.

Becks hisses in my ear, 'Calvi's on the North coast of Corsica. There's got to be a ferry to Marseille.'

'Are you going to do Geography at A-Level?'

'I … '

Her next words are drowned in the explosion of gun fire from the woods on our left. We throw ourselves to the floor. The driver returns a volley of swear words. Suddenly we're going a lot faster. The next Z-bend is around a quarter of a mile away, carved out in the darkness by the blazing headlamps.

The truckie's foot pumps the brake pedal. Nothing happens. He grabs my arm. 'Les freins! Ils sont foutus! Prends le volant!'

I slither across him as he leans to grasp the gearshift with both hands. 'Did he say ...?'

Becks yells, 'Yes! The brakes are buggered! You've got to steer, Joe!'

I grab the wheel. It jumps around in my hands like an angry python. They must have shot through the brake lines. So Bertolini still wants to make our untimely deaths look like an accident. Only a few hundred yards to go. How the hell do I steer a thirty tonner round a hairpin with no brakes?

The truckie reels off instructions to Becks, as he wrestles with the gearshift. There's a thump, a roar from the engine and we're jerked forward as the truck slows to around 30 mph. Now Truckie's lost interest in the gears. Grabbing a rifle from under the seat, he throws himself across to the passenger window and blasts shot after shot off into the night. Becks grabs the gearshift and battles with it. We're two hundred yards before a turn so sharp, it looks like the end of the road.

I shout at Becks, 'We're still going too fast! Get it into a lower gear!'

'I can't hold it in this one!'

'Use your feet!'

Becks swears like the trucker but in Anglo Saxon. She rams herself back into the seat and fires a two-footed kick at the gear shift. It slams into first. There's a horrible crashing of metal on metal. The engine sounds like it's going to explode. The cab almost leaps into the air and we're thrown forwards. Less than a hundred yards to go. The steering wheel is thrashing around in my hands.

Then I feel a huge yank as the trailer unit starts trying to overtake us. Tyres scream as the massive load pushes us towards the bend and that endless drop. The cab veers. We're going to jack knife. Truckie is still firing out of the window like that's going to sort everything out.

The bend is nearly on us. I remember the chicane I drove with Monsieur, where you have to turn the wheel the opposite way you normally would if you want to come out in one piece. I want to steer left. I throw the wheel right. We're jerked backwards. Suddenly that giant weight isn't pushing us anymore. It's pulling. The load's flipped round at a right angle to the cab. I fling the wheel left. But the steering's dead. The rear wheels must be heading for the drop. Taking us with them.

The cab starts to tilt. Truckie's stopped firing. He slides back onto Becks and me like a drink-sodden Sumo wrestler. The cab creaks and takes a steeper angle. I turn off the engine. 'We have to get out!'

Becks' voice is muffled beneath the trucker's dead weight as she screams, 'Monsieur, descendez! Autrement vous allez mourir!'

The thought of dying presses the right button for Truckie. He heaves himself towards the door of the cab and pushes it open. The floor goes more vertical. Becks and I scramble after him and I give his backside a giant shove. He slides out and we fall on top of him.

Completely blocking the road, the cab rears up into the night, headlamps beaming towards the stars. Then it just stays there, rocking gently. The trailer wheels must have caught on some rocks. No telling how long it'll stay like this.

The trucker climbs out from beneath us. Shoving his hand into his back pocket he takes out a pack of Gauloises, lights up and looks at his lorry, as it swings slowly over the drop. I get an uneasy feeling that he's seen this before. He fishes out his mobile, stabs at the buttons and talks rapidly in Corsican French.

I look at Becks. 'Is this our exit cue?'

She whispers, 'I don't know … I can't make out what he's saying …'

Truckie shuts down the call and looks at us. Maybe he looks a bit more closely than he did before. 'Mes amis viennent. Tout va s'arranger.'

His friends are coming. It's all going to be fine. He sits down by the roadside like he's waiting for the AA. Nervously we sit down too, watching the cab's headlights as they swing towards the stars then down again. A rumble of stones comes from the cliff face. Creaking, the truck shifts a couple of feet backwards. Minutes tick by.

Then there's a kind of snarling noise next to us. I jump a mile high, thinking it could be one of Baldy's bears. But it's Truckie, snoring in a wine-soaked sleep.

Becks whispers, 'Know what? I'd like to see his friends before they see us.'

We creep away round to the downhill side of the truck and tuck ourselves into the bushes. Seconds later, headlamps beam round the corner. The black Porsche Carrera rolls slowly down the slope. It stops, unable to go any further. Before a door of that car opens, we're gone.

—॥॥—

All the rest of the night, we stumble on down the mountain. One car passes us going up and it isn't a Porsche. Nothing comes down. The road must have stayed well blocked.

Dawn is trailing grey clouds over the horizon and the road is levelling out, when we see a bus stop. All on its own on this empty road, no houses in sight.

Becks tries to read the tiny, faded timetable that's nailed to the post. '101: Calvi. What's the time?'

'Half six.'

'Another half hour and we could get a lift to Calvi that isn't a truck or a Porsche.'

We sit on the ground, half asleep in the hot rising sun. Right on time, the bus arrives in a cloud of dust.

'Le port de Calvi c'est combien, Monsieur?'

'Douze euros les deux.' The driver doesn't blink an eye at our bedraggled state. He must be used to students falling off mountains. I fumble for Monsieur's envelope, and produce the cash.

There's only one other passenger on the bus. It's an old lady in a black skirt and shawl, clutching something to her chest beneath the shawl. She murmurs to it soothingly. I kind of assume it's a baby. Maybe she's looking after it for her daughter or son. We sit down opposite her and sleep is coming down fast. But I'm sure I haven't dozed off when I hear a comfortable clucking. I've never heard a baby make that kind of noise. I prise my eyelids open. And I could swear the old lady's cuddling a chicken. I stare, but it still looks like a chicken's head and beak I can see above her arm. I look at Becks but she's dozed off. Then I must have done too.

Next thing, the bus driver is yelling at us, 'Ici le port!'

Chicken Woman's gone. Maybe she's taking her beloved hen to market. I don't want to think about that.

Becks and I make our way unsteadily to the ferry. I take her hand, wondering if everyone in Corsica except us, the bus driver and the chicken woman is a bandit.

'God, Joe, you're so cold. Are you alright?'

'Yeah. But I don't think the chicken is.'

She stares at me then pulls me towards the ticket office. 'Low blood sugar. It's time we ate.'

CHAPTER 8

White Horses, Dark Shadows

'You're never going to get through all those croissants.'

'Bet?'

Becks yawns. 'Too tired. Can we go find a deck chair soon?'

Twelve croissants and four coffees later, we head out of the crowded cafeteria. Up on deck, a warm wind is blowing gently. Everyone's settling down for the eleven-hour voyage. Backpackers drag headphones out of their rucksacks. Small children curl up on their parents' laps. Next to us, an old guy puts on his slippers and stows his sandals in a carrier bag. He's got to be English. Becks' eyes close the minute she sits down.

I fumble in my pocket for my mobile. This time, at last, Monsieur answers. 'I received your message. Where are you, Joe?'

'On the ferry from Calvi to Marseille. We're due to arrive at one o'clock tomorrow morning. A lot of stuff's happened, Monsieur. Have you heard from Arnaud?'

'Nothing. And you say he is very ill?'

'Give me a few seconds, Monsieur. Too many people.'

Every muscle creaking, I walk slowly to the stern of the ferry. The propellers churn out a plumy wake, lit by the sinking sun. No one seems to be around now, but I still whisper. 'Arnaud had been trying to get off the drugs. Then Bertolini saw and took the money away from him. He went on the run. We put him on a flight to Marignane. He said he was going to a place called Heimat …?'

'If he said Heimat he's not heading for L'Étoile, thank God. He has bought us some precious time to find him before Bertolini does.'

'Where is Heimat, Monsieur?'

'I will tell you, Joe, when there is time. And when we are not being listened to. Come very quickly to the car. I will be just outside.'

I wander back and collapse into a deck chair next to Becks. As soon as I sit down, all my bones instantly seem to separate themselves into small pieces. I can't help drifting into a wonderful, croissant-stuffed sleep. No dreams at all.

—⁂—

Ten hours later, we're squashed in the queue waiting to get off the boat. I keep a close eye on Becks this time.

'Where are we going with Monsieur? Is Heimat some village where they're sheltering Arnaud?'

I whisper, 'I don't know. Keep your voice down, Becks, and your eyes wide open.'

'Have you seen someone?'

'No, but that doesn't mean a thing.'

We're among the first in the queue as we don't have any bags to collect. People are moving slowly through the gate where officials are inspecting passports. Then I see a dude who looks like police, shoving his way towards us from the back. He's in a dark blue uniform and people are giving way to him, parents grabbing their kids.

We're next through the gate. Becks has seen him too. We hand over our passports and they get looked at and handed back. Dude who looks like police is just behind us now. He shouts, 'Arrêtez!'

The guy in Passport Control is looking at the uniform. I'm looking at the gun. 'Go, Becks!'

We tear out of the gate. The Merc convertible waits, engine running, door open. We throw ourselves inside and Monsieur accelerates sharply away. He takes a back street route out of Marseille like he's got a map of the city in his head. We get to traffic lights just going on red. A police car yodels from our left. He floors the accelerator and we shoot across.

This is a different Monsieur from the drawn, tired figure we last met in that shadow-filled room. The Armani suit's been replaced with black jeans and open necked shirt, sleeves rolled up ready for action. He seems to have a new energy now. It must be the hope of getting his son back.

We nod off, waking to find a flat landscape around us. The Merc bumps down a rutted track, crashing through potholes. Drifts of cloud trail across the night sky, with a moon peeping out. Sometimes, I see the moonlight reflecting off water. 'Any idea where we are?'

She says sleepily, 'I think this could be the Camargue.'

'What's that?'

'Remember Slimbridge? Like, tame wetland?'

'Downy Duckling Days?'

'Think wild wetland that's way bigger. No downy ducklings.'

The sky's slowly getting lighter. Thin strips of gold gleam through the dark clouds on the horizon. Just when I'm beginning to think that the Merc suspension will never be the same again after this trip, the headlamps pick out something that looks like a large shed. It has a thatched roof and no windows. Curving bull horns arch over the door.

Monsieur gets out and gives a low whistle like the call of a bird. The door opens and a guy about my age comes out. He has shoulder length black hair and dark eyes, like Arnaud, and he wears a white baggy shirt and loose black jeans. He gives a slight bow to Monsieur and they shake hands. Monsieur talks to him in a low voice and he nods. 'D'accord, Monsieur le Comte. Tout est prêt.'

Becks whispers to me, 'Monsieur le Comte?'

'That's what he said.'

The young guy walks a few yards out onto the marshes, and gives another of these bird call whistles. 'Mistral, Soleil, Ouragan, venez!'

Distant hooves thud in a steady rhythm. Three pale shapes with flying manes and tails gallop across the water and reeds towards us. The white horses stop and lean friendly heads towards the young man who called them. He pats their necks, talking to them affectionately. Then he goes back into this little house and comes out with bridles.

Monsieur brings saddles. 'Can either of you ride a horse?'

Becks says 'Yes', at the same time as I say, 'No.'

Monsieur looks at Becks as she climbs on board. 'You have the youngest horse, Becks. Ouragan.'

'Hurricane?'

He nods. 'When we gallop, Ouragon will want to go the fastest. Are you comfortable with that?'

'I'm cool, Monsieur. As long as he doesn't do cliffs.'

'He does and we will, but not at a gallop.'

Becks stares at her horse and then at Monsieur. He turns to me. 'You say you have not ridden before, Joe?'

'When I was a little kid my mum took me and my brother a few times. But I fell off a lot.'

In the gathering light I think I can see some mischief in Monsieur's smile. 'Then falling off is not something you will need to practice, is it Joe? Allons-y!'

His friend hoists me into the saddle of the horse called Soleil. Monsieur swings onto Mistral's back like he's ridden all his life. And we're on our way. Soleil splashes happily across marshland that no four wheel drive could negotiate without getting stuck. But I've no idea how to drive this horse. He's on auto-pilot, following Mistral.

I'm trying to remember how to hold the reins when Monsieur brings his horse alongside me. 'Have you ever watched cowboy movies, Joe?'

'One or two …'

'This is the same riding style. Reins in one hand, steer on the neck and sit right down in the saddle.'

As soon as I copy Monsieur my white horse starts to do a little dance. I've found the accelerator and the steering wheel. Not the brakes yet but what the hell. I let out a laugh, 'Allons-y!' He laughs too, it's the first time I've ever heard him laugh, and he tears off on Mistral.

'Move over, loser!' Becks and Ouragan blast up alongside me and Soleil, kicking muddy water all over us. I'm not sure if she's in control or the horse is but she's grinning.

'You wish!' I squeeze my legs into Soleil's sides and get a turbo-charged leap forwards that almost shunts me off into the mud.

We're all three galloping side by side now, as the whole sky slowly explodes with light. Monsieur calls across to me with a quick smile, 'You ride almost as well as you drive, Joe!'

'This beats the Bentley, Monsieur!'

He laughs again. I think, 'I'll always remember this', as we storm across the marshes with a sky of gold blazing behind us.

Then Monsieur holds out his hand in a Slow Down gesture and I have no idea where the brakes are. I wonder if Soleil does voice recognition. 'Lentement, Soleil! Please?' We're still galloping. So I try just sitting right down. Suddenly we're doing a trot so bouncy I nearly lift off; then we're walking. Phew.

Becks is belting round in a huge circle to slow down Ouragan. I grin as I see her nearly go skywards with the trot. She pulls up beside me, breathless. 'We've got company.'

Three riders on white horses are cantering towards us. They're in short black jackets and white shirts, wearing narrow-rimmed black hats, like cowboys on a solemn occasion. Each of them carries a fork with long handles and three curving prongs.

Monsieur raises his right hand. 'Salut, les Guardiens!'

They raise their tridents as their leader replies, 'Salut, Monsieur le Comte!'

Monsieur rides up to them and we can see him deep in conversation. They're nodding and the leader gestures away from us, holding out his trident like a pointer. Then they all wheel their horses round and gallop off westwards.

Monsieur waves us up beside him and we continue our journey at a walk, while the horses stretch their necks on a loose rein. We've been walking like this for maybe an hour when I see some dark shapes in the distance, grazing on the marshland. They look like black cows at first. Then I notice that they're not cows. There's six of them, they have long curving horns and they're definitely bulls. Not that big, but bulls all the same.

Becks hasn't seen them. She's chatting to her horse, not getting much in the way of a reply. As we get closer, these bulls raise their heads and look at us. Then they all start to walk across to us, heads nodding – or is it horns being lowered to charge? I feel nowhere near as relaxed as Monsieur looks. 'Those are bulls, aren't they?'

He just smiles infuriatingly. 'You are most observant, Joe.'

'Well, there's six of them and three of us and …'

'The black bulls of the Camargue will not harm us. Not while we are riding the white horses that the Guardiens use to herd them with those tridents you saw.'

He looks at the bull that's come almost right up to him, and Mistral is as calm as he is. 'These magnificent animals are a rare breed. We have bull running festivals, where young Camargue men have to pick off a cockade fixed between the horns.'

Becks frowns. 'Not like the bull fights in Spain …?'

'No, Becks. We do not kill them as they do in Spain. We celebrate the bravest bulls with statues instead. It is a Camarguais tradition that goes back to beyond the sixteenth century.'

'Statues for bulls! Sweet.'

All through the day we walk and canter across the marshland. The sun rises higher and starts to beat down. Monsieur reaches into his saddle bag and passes us flasks of water. I wonder about asking him how far there is to go but think better of it. As time passes, he seems more and more preoccupied.

The sun's starting to drop towards the horizon when Becks trots Houragon up beside me and Soleil, while Monsieur rides on ahead. She says quietly, 'He seems to know this place so well.'

'Maybe he lived here, once.'

'Did he ever mention it when you were working for him in Bristol?'

'He never talked much about himself.' Is that sound in my head, or … ? Becks looks up. It's not in my head. 'Monsieur! Bertolini has a copter!'

In an instant we're at full gallop, following him towards a lonely outcrop of trees. How easily these white horses can be seen against the black marshland.

The copter's about eight hundred feet above us as we take cover. Among the trees, the horses snort and toss their heads. The copter hovers for a moment, then lifts higher and follows the setting sun. Becks and I exchange worried looks while it becomes a black speck in the sky.

'We will have shelter soon, my friends.' Monsieur doesn't sound quite as relaxed as before.

—⁓—

As we ride on, listening out now for the return of those rotors, a shape starts to appear on the horizon. At first I think it's a mountain range. But as we get closer, it begins to look like a huge rocky outcrop that goes on for miles to either side, white craggy cliffs rising straight up out of the flat plain.

The sun is dropping below the cliff walls, when we see another of these strange little huts. I can smell something that makes my mouth water. Monsieur dismounts and takes off Mistral's saddle and bridle.

I slide off Soleil and I can't move my legs at all. They feel like stone. Becks is grimacing too. 'We'll just have to eat standing up.'

We unsaddle our horses and hobble painfully into the hut. A pot filled with a bubbling stew is hung over slow flames that go quietly up the chimney. Monsieur dishes out huge bowlfuls. 'Eat, my friends. Enjoy the gourmet meat from the black bulls of the Camargue.'

I wonder if it's going to bother Becks that it's a Camargue tradition to eat these bulls as well as making statues of them. But she limps towards her supper even faster than me. We lower ourselves, creaking, to the floor. Grab the bowls and stuff our bellies with the sweet-tasting meat, dipping pieces of baguette into the juice.

Monsieur sits and eats with us. Then he puts his bowl to one side, near the fireplace with its slow flames. 'You remember the first word Arnaud used when he said where he was going?'

Becks says, 'Heimat. It isn't a French word is it, Monsieur?'

'Heimat is German for homeland. Many hundreds of years ago, my ancestors had their origins here, in the Camargue. The family of La Rochelle lived in a walled citadel, high up above the plains.'

'On top of those cliffs?'

'The settlement of Les Baux de Provence. It is a fortress town from mediaeval times, much of it built into solid rock. These days, it is much admired by tourists because of its antiquity and, some say, its beauty. But there are places in Les Baux that do not have a beautiful past.'

'Like those slave tunnels beneath Bristol?'

He looks into the quiet flames. 'Like those slave tunnels, Joe.'

Becks asks, 'So why is L'Étoile now your family home, Monsieur?'

His voice grows colder. 'In those days it was tribal, warlord against warlord. My family held Les Baux for centuries until they were betrayed by one of their own sons, who had been bribed by a rival warlord. That son sacrificed almost his entire family in a night of utter butchery, where tiny children were slaughtered without mercy.'

Becks whispers, 'They killed children?'

Monsieur nods slowly. 'The youngest son escaped and made a new life. He and his offspring built the Chateau de l'Étoile. They established the vineyard from which, hundreds of years later, my family's wine business grew. They never returned to Les Baux. But there were many in the Camargue who always carried a torch for my family. Many who still do, after all this time.'

'The riders – did they sort this food for us? Who are they, Monsieur?'

'The Guardiens have kept the Camargais traditions going for centuries. They safeguard the black bulls of the Camargue. They breed the white horses of the sea, as they are called. And they try to preserve the way of life here.'

He takes a sip of water. 'The Guardiens have always been allied to my family. When I was a little boy, barely able to walk, they taught me to ride. I used to stay with them in their cabanes, just like this one. The bulls horns over the door are there to keep evil spirits away, they say. To me, it is always a sign that I can find a friend, shelter and a horse.'

Becks says, 'So, are the Guardiens looking out for Arnaud until we can get to him, Monsieur?'

He's silent for a time, looking at the flames that are

slowly dying down now. 'They have taken him where he wished to go, to Les Baux. He is in a place of safety, for the time being. But the Guardiens are concerned. For many days now, they have seen men who they say are not tourists. They have told me that the drugs trade has reached Les Baux. It means that Bertolini and his kind have eyes and ears here, as well as me. That is why we are not driving. They will be watching the road to the citadel.'

'So that could have been Bertolini's copter, couldn't it?'

Monsieur looks at us steadily. I tell him everything that happened after he drove us to Marignane airport. When I describe Bertolini's mountain hideaway and what happened there, his eyes harden. 'And I thought I was sending you both out of harm's way. I could not have been more wrong!'

It's then that I know for dead certain that Monsieur had nothing to do with the deal that was going to bring me back to Bertolini. And it reminds me of something else. 'That night, Monsieur. The knife. It wasn't Arnaud.'

I tell him about the throwaway remark from Bertolini's driver during our meeting in the church. 'It must have been one of Bertolini's crew who sent the fake text message and threw the knife.'

In the light of the dying embers of the fire, Monsieur's face shows no emotion. He takes a stick and stirs the glowing wood until sparks dance around.

'Did you know about Bertolini's place at Vivario, Monsieur?'

'No, I did not. I am not surprised that he never told

me. If he had, I would have passed that information to the police. As it is … that task may be yours instead, Joe. It could be a while before we three eat together again.' He stands. 'And now we must sleep for a few hours. There is bedding at the back of the hut. I will tether the horses.' He slips outside and we hear the bird call whistle again.

Becks and I reach for the straw mats and rough blankets. She whispers, 'What did he mean – it could be a while?'

'I don't know. It's like there's something on his mind that he's not telling us.'

'I'm scared, Joe.'

I stare at her. 'That's a first!'

'No, I don't mean for us. I'm scared for Monsieur. Like something horrible's going to happen to him and he knows what it is.'

I roll myself up in the itchy blanket. 'Well, whatever it is, we'll just have to do something about it!'

CHAPTER 9

Comeback

There are no stars in the sky as we ride at a walk across the marshes towards Les Baux. A heavy layer of cloud shuts out everything. We don't need to see; the horses pick their way easily through the water and reeds.

After about an hour, the ground starts to rise steeply and the horses' hooves tap on rock. Soleil's shoulders and hind legs push hard as we climb. His head goes down with the effort and I give him a loose rein. We're on a road that seems to have been bombed out of the cliff face, as though a giant has hit it casually with his pen knife. To the right and left are solid rock walls. Strange shapes rear up dimly in the darkness either side of us.

We climb steadily upwards. A wind is starting to blow, more fiercely as we get higher. None of us says anything. We don't know who might be listening. I look up, and above me in the dark night, I can vaguely make out the jagged heights of this fortress town that was built so many hundreds of years ago.

We get to a stone archway that looks like it once might have been an entrance gate. Monsieur dismounts, hitches up the stirrups, ties the reins beneath them and signals to us to do the same. Then he gives the horses a gentle shove on their rumps, saying quietly to them, 'Écoutez.' Listen out. The three white horses turn their heads towards him, ears flicking backwards and forwards. Then they walk off into the darkness.

We follow Monsieur quietly into this ghost town. There's no sign of any inhabitants. We go past cafes and shops that sell all kinds of your usual tourist stuff. Each one is closed and silent.

Becks touches my arm. She's gazing at a large building that looks like it was once important, though it's so old and wind-ridden that no one could live in it now. On the porch are the battered remains of a sixteen-point star engraved into the stonework, just like the star on Monsieur's front door. He sees us looking at it. 'The emblem of my family. This was once their chateau, before the betrayal when the children were killed.'

He walks on. We're slipping quietly down streets where there's nothing but ruins, ancient buildings that house no one. It's eerily silent, no sound but our footsteps and the dull, whining wind. Becks touches my arm again. We're both getting the same feeling that she had when we were getting out of Aix. I whisper to Monsieur, 'Someone's here.'

'I know. But we must go on. There is no choice now, Joe.'

We reach a block of ruins where time and the merciless Mistral wind have put in some heavy punishment. Monsieur walks quietly over to a building with a huge stone window. The window's glassless like all the rest and it's totally black to look through, so empty of everything. The clouds are slowly starting

114

to part, and the starlight shines on the top beam of the window. There's a date carved into the ancient stone, wind blasted and just visible. 1571. And the words, Post Tenebras Lux.

'What do those words mean, Monsieur?'

He's looking up at them too. 'They say a rich nobleman had them engraved here as a memorial of that terrible night. It is Latin; After Darkness, Light. Because one could only pray for light after such a dreadful darkness. Arnaud was always moved by those words when we used to come to Les Baux, before I lost him.'

He turns to us. 'Now listen carefully both of you. We will go in together to Arnaud. If anything happens, you must not look for me. You must get him out and away. You know the names of the horses; call them, and they will come. The Guardiens are waiting. They will soon be at your side.'

He starts to descend a flight of stone steps into the ruin. We follow him, into a blackness where I'm trying to make out shapes. We're at the bottom of the steps now, in a corridor. I can dimly see an open door that's swinging on iron hinges, creaking in the wind.

Monsieur moves along the corridor without a sound, almost invisible now.

Becks whispers, 'I have such an awful feeling about that door.'

'So let's keep right up with him!'

Pushing the door slowly open, Monsieur goes through. We tiptoe after him and see just a shadow, standing motionless in the darkness. I can't hear him breathing. We look around, expecting an ambush at any time, but nothing and no one moves. All we can hear is the relentless wind blowing through the empty stone windows; and that creaking door.

Monsieur whispers, 'Arnaud, mon fils, tu me reconnais?'

The last direction I would ever have looked is upwards. A flying figure drops from the rafters, staggers as he hits the floor and falls into his father's waiting arms.

—∞—

For a few seconds, time stands still, as Monsieur holds his son again after so long. Then, we go silently out of that room with its restless door, along the dark corridor, and up the steps. Becks and I tiptoe on ahead to the top of the steps and stare into the shadowy streets.

She catches her breath, 'I thought I saw ...'

'What?'

'Something moving, in that doorway.'

We strain our eyes at the doorway but can't see anything.

Monsieur calls the white horses just once, in a voice so low I think they'll never hear above this whining wind. There's a long pause. We look at the pools of shadow in the doorways of these ruined buildings, expecting to hear a gunshot or see a silver knife flash out towards us. Then, three pale shapes come out of the night. Their bare hooves tap on the cobbled road while their heads nod and reach towards us. They don't make a sound as we unhitch the stirrups and reins.

While Becks climbs onto Ouragon, Monsieur helps Arnaud up in front of me onto Soleil. Then he's on Mistral and we head back through these deserted streets. They're nowhere near as dark as we'd like them to be. The night sky is almost clear of cloud now, and the stars sparkle like ice particles in the moaning wind. To make things worse, a huge full moon is starting to clear the horizon. The silver light blazes across the stretches of marshland, glinting on the streaks of water far below.

Monsieur rides ahead of us, quickly glancing back from time to time. I have one arm round Arnaud to keep him on board. His head drops forward sometimes, like he's going to pass out. I can feel his ribs, he's so thin. 'Are you OK, Arnaud? Can you hear me?'

He murmurs, 'It is so good to see you both again, Joe. My father …' His voice falters.

'Hang on in there, Arnaud. We're going to get you out of here!'

Becks leans over and whispers in my ear, 'Why hasn't Monsieur got Arnaud with him on his horse?'

I whisper back, 'Soleil is the biggest and strongest, isn't he?'

We ride through the old archway. The road starts to drop steeply as we begin the descent towards the marshes. The wind's getting quieter as we go down the rocky track. The horses feel their way delicately with their unshod hooves.

Those weird rock shapes loom over us again. They're like frozen, battered giants, watching this convoy of white horses and quiet riders slipping away from the dark, haunted citadel.

As the road starts to level out and rock gives way to marshes, Monsieur motions us up beside him. 'Remember what I said. If anything happens, get Arnaud out of here. Do not look for me. Stay with the Guardiens – they are close to us now.' Then he pushes Mistral quickly into a trot and goes on ahead.

Becks looks at me. 'I don't understand …'

I stare across the stretches of mud and reeds and at the rippling water that's reflecting the huge, glowing moon. I can't make out any sign of the Guardiens.

That distorted reflection of the moon is the last thing I see before a sharp crack almost blows out my eardrums. Soleil takes a huge leap to one side. I hang on desperately. When I look up, Mistral is on his hind legs. He's neighing, a horrible, high-pitched scream. And Monsieur is falling.

Then it all happens like a DVD in Fast Forward. More bullets fly around us. Black riders on white horses come out of nowhere. One of them grabs Soleil's rein, and we go into a flat out gallop. I hold onto Arnaud and grip Soleil's sides as he leaps reeds and ditches, his legs moving so fast that I have to hang onto his mane.

Monsieur must have known this was going to happen. And the one thing he asked us to do was get his son out of it. When all I want to do is go back and get him out of it too. This huge moonlit sky is crashing all around me. Because I know that Monsieur could stay on a rearing horse like second nature.

Becks gallops up alongside us. 'I'm going back for Monsieur!'

I shout to the Guardien who's grabbed Soleil's rein

and is pulling us relentlessly onwards, 'Il faut chercher Monsieur! Arrêtez! Arrêtez!'

He calls back, 'Monsieur le Comte nous a donné ses commandes! On doit sauver le fils!'

'I'm going back, Joe. Take care of Arnaud!' Becks turns Ouragon and rides off into the night, towards the explosions of gunfire behind us.

'For God's sake, Becks …!'

We're not galloping out into the marshes. We're doing a huge semi-circle around the cliffs and into a rocky place. I can still hear gun shots behind us. There's an agonised cry from one of the riders. They must be trying to engage these gunmen to stop them following us. Trying with the only weapons they have – the speed and agility of their horses, a deep knowledge of this place and the tridents they use to herd and protect the black bulls of the Camargue.

The gun shots are behind us now. They get fainter as we ride on into this dark place, where rocks rise all around us. Some are at crazy angles, with shapes that look nothing like anything the wind could have done. I can make out one rock that looks like an alligator towering up onto its back feet. Another is like a giant's grinning head, with holes where the eyes should be.

The white horses have slowed to a cautious walk. We're in a deep valley below the citadel. This is not an easy place to ride; the horses pick their way over slippery stone. It looks like an ancient cemetery with these tall rocks rearing their heads around us. I know why we've come here. There's cover. There wouldn't be any out on those flat marshes. Not with the merciless blaze of this

119

full moon and the sky full of stars, all the clouds blown away. The wind has dropped to a whisper. Arnaud's head is heavy on my shoulder; I can hear his short, shallow breaths.

We head beneath a group of trees, well out of range and sight of those gunmen. The Guardien still holds Soleil's reins.

'Où est-ce que nous sommes?'

He says quietly, 'Le Val d'Enfer.' I knew at the time that 'Le Val' means The Valley. I only learned afterwards that Le Val d'Enfer means The Valley of Hell.

We must be at least a mile from that first gun shot, here in the shades. The Guardien leans across from his horse and speaks to Arnaud in a low voice. Arnaud shakes his head like he's dreaming nightmares, then slumps forward again. 'Je sais … mon père …'

Another of the Guardiens approaches us, leading a white horse. It's Mistral. He looks unhurt. I feel numb, as DI Wellington's voice echoes in my head. 'Organisations like this never forget. They're a kind of Mafia.' How savagely Bertolini must have wanted the blood of the man who completely destroyed his UK drug running operation.

A steady thud of rotor blades cuts through the night. Green and red lights and a flashing white light lift off across the marshes in the distance.

The Guardien who grabbed the reins is looking at the copter too. Now I can see that it's the same guy who brought us the horses to ride to Les Baux. He says quietly, tears bright in the moonlight on his face, 'Vendetta.'

We walk the horses on together, out of the Val

120

d'Enfer and back onto the marshes. As we ride on, more Guardiens join us on their white horses. There must be twenty of them by the time we pass the cabane where Becks and I ate our last meal together with Monsieur. They form a kind of guard around me and Arnaud, on my tireless Soleil. Their leader circles around them, exchanging words, keeping an eye out.

I whisper, 'Can you still hear me, Arnaud?'

His voice is dull. 'They have taken him …'

'If they have, we're going to get him back!'

About an hour into the ride there's a thunder of hooves behind us. Two Guardiens gallop up and exchange rapid French with the leader. I overhear the words, 'On a cherché partout … rien.'

Then Becks pulls up alongside us. I look at her. She just shakes her head, and buries her face in Ouragan's thick white mane.

—⁓—

The razor-sharp stars fade into a stormy dawn. The sun creeps up from the horizon, sending dark gold rays through black clouds. We walk on steadily, lashed by rain showers.

When we stop to let the horses drink and graze, the Guardiens give us water, bread and a kind of hard dry salami that tastes a lot better than it looks. Little is said. When they do speak to us, their voices are rough but kind. The dark eyes in sun-browned faces look with sadness at Arnaud.

The food and water untouched beside him, he sits

121

alone, near where Soleil is grazing peacefully. He stares at the ground. I can guess what he's seeing. I want to go over to him. But I don't know what to say.

Becks is sat next to me. She grabs a fistful of grass and yanks it up. I watch as she gets up stiffly, goes to Ouragan and holds out her hand. He takes the grass delicately in his mouth. She strokes his neck. Then she turns and looks at me. And suddenly we're back in the chateau on the night of the silver knife. When that familiar voice in the back of my mind told me what we had to do for Monsieur. I nod slowly at her. I don't feel so tired now. Because I know it's what Dad would do for his old friend, if he was able to.

'Allons, mes amis!' The Guardien leader calls us back to our horses and the convoy moves on.

When we arrive at the cabane where we set off for Les Baux, Monsieur's Merc is still parked there. The rider leading me and Arnaud gets off his horse. A woman is at the door, in a long black skirt and white blouse. She hugs Rider; I think she must be his mother. He talks quickly in French. I can't catch a word. But I hear her say, with such tenderness in her voice as she looks at Arnaud, 'Le pauvre, le pauvre petit.'

She comes over to us and Arnaud slides off Soleil into her arms. She and Rider half carry him into the cabane. Becks and I unsaddle, hug our brave horses and say Goodbye to them. They wander off swishing their tails, like it's all in a night's work.

The other Guardiens salute Madame then they melt away into the marshes. I wonder if the rider who cried out is still alive. But maybe we'll never know.

It's getting dark. We can smell food again as we enter the cabane. Another pot bubbles over quiet flames. Rider's mother watches Arnaud as he gulps down the stew. She hands him a baguette. He tears a piece off, dips it into that sweet-smelling juice and devours it like a hungry animal. She glances across at us, smiles and fills three more bowls from the pot, passing them to us with more bread.

Swaying slightly with the sleep that's catching up with him fast, Arnaud looks at Becks. 'Is there any news of my father?'

She shakes her head. 'We looked everywhere for him, Arnaud. That's got to be good news. If they've taken your father he must still be alive.'

Arnaud says in a dead voice, 'Bertolini will torture him, for days, maybe weeks. Then, he will kill him.' The shockingly matter-of-fact words hang in the air.

'I think I know where they've taken him.'

He stares at me.

'It's a long story. I'll tell you tomorrow. On the way.'

I can see there's half a million questions Arnaud wants to ask, but his eyes are closing. He thanks Madame briefly as she pulls a horsehair blanket over him, and he crashes out on the straw mat.

Rider's mother passes us a jug of water. She talks quietly to Rider and shows him that she has the keys of Monsieur's car. He nods and she goes outside. We hear the sound of the Merc starting up. Madame has gone to hide Monsieur's car.

We eat together, Becks, Rider and I, passing bread and the jug of water to each other. Arnaud sleeps, motionless and silent.

Rider holds out his hand to us across the slow flames of the fire. He says simply, 'Michel.' We grab his hand in turn.

'Joe.'

'Becks.'

He tells us about the man he loves like a father. About Monsieur le Comte de la Rochelle. Michel and Arnaud were childhood friends, learning to ride together on the Camargue. When Michel's father got very ill, Monsieur had him cared for until he died. Michel says he would do anything to help get Monsieur back.

'Vraiment? Tu es avec nous? You're with us?'

'I am with you!'

'So, we're four, as long as Arnaud can get some strength back. I'm not sure that's enough.'

'It might have to be enough, Joe!'

'Half a sec while I phone a friend.'

He picks up first go. 'Joe. You OK? Saw the news that time.'

'I'm good, Lenny. How's Jamie?'

'No job still. Not after that.'

'Would you like to help me and some mates send Bertolini to the place where he should never have put your brother, Lenny?'

'Yeah. Good. How?'

'You have to fly to France and get to Marseille ferry port, fast. Can you do that?'

'Jamie'll fix it.'

'I'll call you tomorrow then.'

'See y'later, Joe.'

CHAPTER 10

Vivario

'I didn't know that Bertolini had this place. I've spent time in Corsica but that was at his mansion on the coast.'

I've watched Arnaud carefully as we eat breakfast the next morning, with Madame brewing up fresh café au lait over the embers of the fire. He looks a whole lot better than he did last night. But I still wonder if he's going to have the strength to go on this mission.

I soon realise that this isn't going to be my choice anyway. He gives me a chance to get half a baguette and a bowl of café au lait inside me, then his eyes are asking mine all those questions. I tell him what happened after he got on the plane.

He gets up with an energy I've not seen in him before and asks Madame to bring the Merc round. 'Have you money for the ferry tickets, Joe?'

I produce the envelope with the remaining wad of fifty pound notes and Euros. 'It's yours. Your dad gave it us.' I hand it towards him.

He shakes his head. 'You must look after the money, Joe.'

As we pile into the Merc, I wonder at Arnaud's acute knowledge of the deadly habit that hasn't left him yet. I wonder at his courage. Not sure if I could have refused such an offer if I was trying to come off cocaine. Now I'm sure he's got the mental strength for what we have to do.

He hands me the keys. 'You must be our driver, Joe. It is a risk, with the police, but nothing compared to the risks we will be taking soon.'

'You better help me then!'

Takes me a while to get used to driving on the right and changing gear with my right hand, but Arnaud is a brilliant coach. Despite all the advice from the back seat.

'There's the sign to Arles, Joe! We went left there so it's got to be a right here.'

'Chill, Becks. Arnaud knows this place, remember?'

I glance sideways at Arnaud, and he gives me that half smile that I know so well. 'You two are quite a team.'

'We're all a team, now. One more to come. And together we're going to get your dad away, Arnaud.'

As we approach Marseille, I pull over and call Lenny.

'Jus' landed, Joe.'

'See you at the ferry port, in the cafe.'

Arnaud says, 'Before we go to the ferry there is some equipment we will need. I know where we can get it.'

We park up and go shopping. Arnaud explains. 'Mobile phones are no use in Corsica. We would never get a signal in the mountains.' We come back with five two-way radios and two powerful torches.

In the cafe, I look around for Lenny. Then I see his familiar shaved head and boxer's face, the scar below his right eye. He moves quickly through the crowded tables towards us and grabs my hand. 'Hey, Joe, s'good!'

'Great to see you, Lenny! Meet Becks, Arnaud, Michel.' They shake. I look at my watch. 'We'll fill you in on the boat. If we get a move on, we'll catch the next sailing for Calvi.'

An hour later we're sat round a table in the ferry eaterie, while Marseille fades on the horizon of the deep blue sea. I've updated Lenny on everything that happened after he warned me not to take the chauffeur's job. Arnaud translates swiftly for Michel, as Lenny tells them how his brother Jamie was set up and jailed as a drug runner, doing the same job as me, by the man who has taken Monsieur.

Arnaud's talking in a low voice, taking quick glances around him now and then. Lenny's aware of the situation too, using even fewer words than usual. We've got the radios and torches stowed out of sight in a hold-all.

Lenny drains his coffee and looks at me. 'You want police in this, Joe?' I can see the wary look in his eyes. Arnaud's, too.

I shake my head. 'Hordes of armed police anywhere near that place is too risky for Monsieur. The job needs to be sorted before we call them in.'

Becks says brightly, 'Oh-my-god there's THE most enormous seagull flying just outside the window!' She gets up and bumps into the chair of a dude sitting at the next table, knocking his café au lait straight into his lap. 'Oh, I am just SO sorry! Here, let me help you mop it up!'

'Ce n'est rien, Mademoiselle …' He's about Baldy's age, but with more hair, and an expensive looking suit.

'Oh, but your poor trousers … have another serviette!'

Lenny grins at my puzzled look. 'Ears too big.'

Becks and suited dude are now totally occupied clearing up the flood of café au lait. Arnaud smiles as he says quietly, 'Go on, Joe.'

'We all know what the big problem is. They shoot people. We may be five against their three, but …'

'Assuming that there are no more than three, Joe.'

'There could be more, I guess …'

'It is harder to shoot people in the dark, Joe.'

'The torches? Is that …?

Lenny says to Arnaud, 'Plan, yeah?'

'Sorry, it's your call, Arnaud. Let's hear it.'

Becks slips back into her seat, eyes bright with victory. Dude in Suit is doing a hobbling walk towards the Men's, holding a wad of serviettes over the massive wet patch on his trousers.

Arnaud continues quietly, 'They will be watching the road, and the airspace above them. We must approach from where they would never expect anyone to come. And it must be from more than one direction.'

He sketches quickly on a serviette. 'I have been to Corsica many times with Bertolini, although never to this mountain fortress. There is a rail tunnel that runs by his hideaway. There is also a railway station at Vivario.'

He looks at Michel. 'Est-ce que tu aimes grimper comme toujours, mon ami?'

Michel smiles and nods. He knows what Arnaud is asking him to do. 'Comme toujours.'

'There are other entrances to the tunnel along the way, for maintenance work. Michel will leave at a lower point than us and climb the cliff. We will aim for the building from higher up. Then we take out the power, we keep in radio contact and we see what can be done to these men with guns when we have darkness on our side.'

I remember Becks and me hanging over that awful drop. 'Doesn't Michel need climbing gear or a buddy or …?'

'Michel used to climb the cliffs of Les Baux before breakfast, in the dark, with no gear at all, just for fun.'

'Right.'

Lenny nods his approval of The Plan. 'S'do it.'

—᠁—

By the time we dock at Calvi it's eleven at night. We go up to the taxi rank.

'Nous sommes cinq. Vivario?' I might as well have said, 'Yo dudes, we're a remote cell of Al Quaeda,' the windows get wound up so fast.

I look at Arnaud. 'Could we get the train?'

'There is only one that runs at night from Calvi to Vivario. It will have left at ten.'

Suddenly, Becks starts sobbing, huge tears rolling down her face. I stare at her. I had no idea she could get so upset about missing a train. I've only ever seen her cry once, when her cat died of old age. That made me cry too.

She goes up to a Fiat six-seater, stumbling and grief-stricken. Stunned, we follow. Taking a quick break from sobbing, she hisses at me, 'Tell them to cry, Joe!'

We're all wiping our eyes with our sleeves as she taps on the driver's window. 'Monsieur, s'il vous plaît! Mes frères! Ce sont les funérailles de notre père à Vivario demain!'

He slowly winds down the window, and glares at Becks and her four broken-hearted brothers. I hope that tears aren't the in thing with the local bandits. Grumbling about it being our father's fault for dying as he was probably a bad man anyway, he lets us get in.

The steep, twisting road that leads up the mountain is quiet. Half an hour later, the taxi pulls up outside the small, deserted railway station in the centre of the village of Vivario. The driver demands two hundred euros in return for this death-defying journey. Michel exclaims under his breath. The Fiat screeches off like the streets are bristling with snipers.

The whole place looks deserted as we jump down onto the tracks and walk into the tunnel. I grab a torch, and Lenny brings up the rear with the other one. We walk on fast through the tunnel, into the darkness. The track goes upwards in a steady rise that slowly becomes steeper.

'At least we haven't got any trains to worry about.'

'What makes you think that, Joe?'

'Well, you said the one train from Calvi to Vivario left at ten.'

'Correct, if it was on time, and they usually are in Corsica. However, there is also the mail train at two in the morning going in the opposite direction, to Calvi.'

'The mail train …'

Becks looks at the narrow gauge track. 'Is it quite a small train, Arnaud?'

'Quite small.'

'But this is quite a narrow tunnel.'

Tunnels have no more novelty value for me and Becks. But trains in tunnels are something else. Around us, we can see walls carved out of the rock glistening in the light of the torches, with small rivulets of moisture trickling down them. As our feet crunch on the stones between the sleepers I can hear something else too. Every now and then there's a light pattering of paws. I shine the torch after the pattering and see a couple of long tails whisk away into the darkness. Michel trips and swears.

'Sorry!' I get the torch back into line.

He just laughs. 'De rien.'

'They were huge!'

Arnaud says, 'They are nothing like as unpleasant as the vermin we will be meeting with soon, Becks.'

'True. They couldn't possibly stink like Bertolini.'

'Ah, here it is! Shine the torch to your left, Joe.'

There's a wider area in the tunnel wall, with lamps, a few spanners and a torque wrench lying on top of two large crates. Behind them, in the wall, is a wooden door. We push the heavy crates to one side and Arnaud tries the door. It doesn't budge.

'Is this where Michel will climb from?'

'If we can open it!'

Lenny throws a massive kick at the door. Splinters fly and the jagged wood parts. Revealing a wall of boulders.

131

Arnaud says calmly, 'It could have been a rock fall. Or it could have been sealed off. No matter, we look for other opportunities.'

We trudge on up, all of us more wary now. At the back, Lenny is flashing the torch behind us.

I whisper, 'If it was a rock fall, wouldn't the rail company have unblocked it, Arnaud?'

'It could have been recent.' But I can guess what he's thinking.

'Hey, guys!' Lenny's holding a small object between finger and thumb. We all gather round as the light from his torch shines on a rifle shell.

Arnaud says quietly, 'So this approach may not be as unexpected as we had hoped. We must now proceed with extreme caution, my friends.'

With small talk silenced, all we're doing now as we walk on upwards is listen for the train. I look at that narrow gauge track, and wonder how much on each side the train will fill up the tunnel.

'Is there another of those wider bits soon?'

'I think there is only a single refuge, as they are called, between one station and the next.'

Becks whispers, 'Have you been on the train, Arnaud?'

'I have travelled on the train, yes.'

'How much room was there outside the carriages?'

'The tunnel walls always looked very close. As though they were just beyond the window glass.'

Now he tells us. Five minutes before the train's due. But something's happening already. Very quietly, the rails are starting to hiss.

'It's around half a kilometre away, going very slowly because of the slope. It always stops for several minutes, the incline is so steep. The first time, I thought it would never get going again.'

'We can't be far away from where the tunnel goes past Bertolini's place.'

We go on up the steep slope, walking faster than before. Still no sign of anywhere to dodge into. The rails are starting to vibrate. The train's got its breath back and is having another go at the slope.

'They call it 'le tremblotant'. Some say because it sways and rattles so much. Others say it's because of the deep ravines you look down on when it's out in the open; enough to make anyone with no head for heights get a bit shaky.'

Arnaud's breathing harder as we all run up the rail track. I hope he's got the stamina for this. We can hear the rumbling sound of a diesel engine in the distance now. I shine the torch around as we take long strides upwards and the rumbling steadily gets louder.

Then we can see a glow of lights behind us. Lenny shines the torch towards the train and gets a long whistle blast in return. But still it comes on, trundling up the slope. I flash my torch around the rock walls either side.

Arnaud shouts, 'Over here!' He jumps across the track to where there's a slight hollow in the tunnel wall. As the rest of us get there, we see a flat panel about four feet high and three feet wide in the hollow; it's the same colour as the rocks, but it looks like wood. No telling how thick it is.

The train's about a hundred yards away now, and we

can make out its shape. The width of the engine unit leaves around four feet either side, but the carriages behind are a much tighter fit.

Arnaud yells, 'Kick it down!'

We all attack the panel with our shoulders and feet. I pray that there's not another solid wall of boulders behind it. Nothing happens. The train's lights are dazzling now, the whistle is going again and its horn is blaring. It's not going to stop or even slow down for us.

Lenny roars, 'WAY!' He and Michel have linked arms, shoulder to shoulder, about to charge. The engine unit is almost on us as the pair of them throw themselves like wild bulls at the door. The engine roars past so close, we can smell diesel fuel and feel the hot blast.

CRUMP! The door disintegrates and we all fall through it on top of each other. The carriages pass, right where we were just now. We instinctively draw our feet back as the train rumbles on upwards through the tunnel, leaving us choking on diesel fumes and blinded by smoke.

I shine the torch. It shows a flight of steps that go upwards in a spiral. Arnaud says quietly, in between trying to muffle coughs that shake his whole body, 'I used to visit the casinos when Bertolini was throwing money at me … if I was back there now, I would bet my last euro that this is his ultimate escape route, if things get too hot for him up there.'

We sit down briefly and make a new battle plan. Arnaud could beat Napoleon at this. He says in a harsh whisper, still trying to get his breath back, 'I was wrong. I never thought that Bertolini would consider the rail tunnel as a line of entry. The fact that he seems to have made it part of his last-ditch escape strategy says to me that he could also be expecting visitors from this direction. Agree?'

We nod.

He's breathing more steadily now. 'It's possible that Bertolini may know that this door has been broken through. So we have to go fast, be prepared for ambush, look out for cameras and avoid them. If we disable them we will be sending a clear message as to where we are. OK?'

We're fine with that. We race up the spiral steps, listening out for any sound of Bertolini's crew. Our torches flash ahead to identify cameras, mikes, infra red beams, anything that could give us away. The walls around us have been hacked out of the rock, but we can see no signs of any wiring that could indicate a security system.

We've been moving rapidly on up for about half an hour. I can hear Arnaud's painful breathing. Then the torch picks out another door in the rocks on our left, while the steep stairway goes on up. Lenny tries the door. To our surprise, it opens easily. I turn the torch onto it. 'This is the route Becks and I took downwards when we got away. The ledge out there goes on towards the front windows of Bertolini's place.'

Lenny says, 'Two better than one. OK, Michel?'

'OK, Lenny.'

Arnaud says, 'Time to check the radios.'

Radios are good. Then Lenny and Michel are gone without a sound out onto the ledge, like a height so huge means nothing to either of them.

Becks, Arnaud and I go quietly on up the steps. Still no sign of cameras or men with guns.

Becks says, 'Look! Another door.'

'I really hope this one opens. We're clean out of stairs.' A rock wall is the only thing ahead of us.

She opens it cautiously. 'We're on the roof.'

Arnaud says softly, 'And there is Bertolini's helicopter.' He swings himself into it and we follow. 'We have to disable it!' Arnaud and I look at the maze of instrument dials and switches.

Becks rummages through the lockers, pulling out life rafts, two way radios, torches – and then a tool box. 'This looks pretty disabling.' She hands a hammer to Arnaud.

With a furious energy he smashes the hammer again and again into the instrument panel, until it's nothing but fragments of printed circuit board and trailing wire.

Arnaud's anger is catching. We're all burning with it now, as we leave the wrecked copter to look for a way into Bertolini's last hiding place. The hammer is still in Arnaud's hand. Becks stuffs a couple of screwdrivers into her pockets. 'You never know …'

We try standing on the steel plate. No response. Scouting around the building we find some steps going down into the rocks towards a door. It's locked. Becks shoves in a screwdriver and levers it up and down. Without much of a fuss, the door opens. I guess they're not expecting your casual thief in this wilderness.

We go quietly into a kitchen that's dimly lit by the wall lights above an oven and dishwasher. There's a fridge so huge you could walk into it, a massive chest freezer and acres of work surfaces that are spotlessly clean.

I whisper, 'We might have to add the cook to the numbers. Can't see Bertolini making his own bacon butties.'

We can hear the thrumming of the generator from not far away. Arnaud calls Michel and Lenny.

Lenny replies. 'On the ledge, big window. Men with guns, drinking brandy.'

'How many?'

'Five.'

'We've taken out his copter. We're in the kitchen near the generator. We take out the power then look for my father.'

'S'good.'

As we walk towards the door at the far end of the kitchen, the sound of the generator gets louder. Arnaud opens the door. The thrumming is deafening now.

Becks wrinkles her nose. 'Smells like nail varnish.'

'It is gas – propane, probably. Highly volatile.'

I know enough from my Physics GCSE that highly volatile means it could explode with maybe just a movement. 'We better not sneeze, then.'

We close the door to the kitchen and I shine the torch around. The generator is inside a large metal box, connected by a pipe with a tap to a cylinder around six feet high and three in diameter that must be supplying the gas.

'We turn off the tap to stop the supply. We wait a few seconds after the generator stops to allow any remaining gas to clear the pipe. Then we smash the pipe so they can't turn the supply back on.'

'And pray like mad that there's no gas left in the pipe.'

'What's in that other box?'

Arnaud and I look where Becks is pointing. He whispers, 'Thank you Becks – I didn't notice it. It must be the backup power supply. Probably kicks in automatically if the main generator goes. We have to knock out both of them, the backup first.'

I shine the torch as Arnaud turns off the tap from the gas cylinder to the backup generator. 'There can be very little gas in this pipe as it's not in use. I'm going to make it useless now.'

He smashes the hammer with three precise blows into the gas pipe, and it breaks away from the tap. Nothing explodes although the smell of nail varnish is stronger. The noise of the main generator is so loud that hopefully no one's heard the hammer. Feeling more nervous now, I shine the torch on the tap to the gas cylinder. Arnaud twists the tap to Off. And we wait.

Lenny calls through. 'Dude going out. Could be coming your way.'

'Hope not.'

'If only the beastly thing would pack up!'

The generator sounds really happy, still rumbling away to itself.

Becks whispers, 'Look out! Someone's coming!'

The brightness around the door to the kitchen suddenly increases as the ceiling lights go on. We take cover behind the generators. Dude in Kitchen hums quietly to himself as he opens a cupboard. There's a rustling, then the unmistakable swish of cereal being poured into a bowl, followed by the glug of milk.

'He's got the munchies. Cute. Bet he has a teddy bear, too.'

The generator stops and it all goes black. I switch off the torch. Our next door neighbour swears loudly in Corsican French.

'I cannot use the hammer while he is in there!'

Crash! Sounds like a mountain of crockery has hit the floor. More swearing then Bump! I think he's going to bring the door down. Another loud Thump, and we hear his footsteps stumbling downstairs in the dark.

From below we can hear more shouting. I switch the torch back on and shine it on the pipe. Arnaud smashes the hammer twice through it, there's a flash of flame as the pipe breaks off then the flame goes out. At the same time we hear a dull Wallop from below.

Becks radios to Lenny and Michel. 'What's happening?'

'Shooters.'

I shine the torch towards the door and we go quickly down the stairs from the kitchen towards the salon. Half way down we see a door on our right. Arnaud opens it and we slip through, closing it behind us just as someone rushes past and up the stairs. We tiptoe down a long, windowless corridor. Then the torch is shining on a solid wall of rock ahead of us. There's just one door to our left. Through the small round pane of glass in the door we can see a dim light that flickers. With all the power off, it must be a candle.

Arnaud's voice is unsteady. 'I am afraid of what we will find.'

'So are we, Arnaud. But we have to go in.'

Arnaud is shaking, like he was in Monsieur's house in Bristol. He must be nearing the end of all his energy now.

Becks whispers, 'Joe and I'll go in first, Arnaud. Your dad might have escaped. He's not the type to let himself get pushed around.'

The door isn't locked. She opens it slowly. There's a candle burning on a small table beside a marble slab. Monsieur is lying there, motionless. Above him there's a small crucifix on the wall, with a figure of the dying Christ, his hands nailed on the cross. The shock makes us stand there completely paralysed as Arnaud brushes past.

Monsieur's eyes are closed, his face is very peaceful. He's still in the black jeans and shirt he wore on our horseback ride to Les Baux. His arms are lying at his side, the hands looking relaxed. He could be asleep. Except that in the light of the candle, his face is deathly pale. There's a deep gash in his forehead, with dark blood that's trickled down towards his eyes, then congealed.

No one's even taken the trouble to wipe away that blood. But someone laid Monsieur out on this marble slab and lit a candle for him. They must really believe that Monsieur is dead. And even murdering, cowardly drug runners give him some respect. As I look at him, so pale and still, I have to think they're right. Monsieur is gone. We've lost him.

I can hear Arnaud's short, shallow breaths as he lifts his father's wrist and feels for a pulse. Then he kneels and lays his head on Monsieur's chest to try and hear a heartbeat. Brings his face right up close to Monsieur's for the feel of any breathing. Finally, wraps his arms around his father as he says slowly and quietly, still kneeling at the marble slab where Monsieur le Comte de la Rochelle is lying motionless, 'Pardonnes-moi, mon père. Je t'aime. Je t'ai toujours aimé.'

There's a silence in this room with its merciless rock walls that goes right into my head like a drumbeat. Becks and I look at Arnaud holding his father in the flickering light of the candle. Then we slip quietly out of the room to give him some cruelly brief moments to say Goodbye.

Lenny calls through. 'You guys OK?'

'We're on our way.'

A shot rings out below, then another. We go back into the room where Arnaud is getting to his feet, swaying slightly. 'I cannot leave here without my father's body.'

'I know. But right now we have some unfinished business if we're going to leave here at all.'

Becks puts her arm round Arnaud and we go quickly back into the corridor. I turn, taking a last quick glance before I close the door. The candle flickers with the flow of air, and the light dances on Monsieur's pale hand. For one vicious, deceptive moment, I think I see a tiny movement in those long fingers, and a huge surge of hope makes my heart stop. Then I think, You idiot, get a grip and face up. It has to be the candlelight. I say nothing to Arnaud. It would be beyond cruel.

We run back along the corridor. Ahead we can hear shouting, and feet thundering back down the stairs from the kitchen to the salon. The corridor's dark, but we can see a dim glow around the door ahead. Arnaud whispers, and I wonder at his calm, so like his father's, 'Must be battery powered lighting that's kicked in. I didn't think of that.'

The feet and the shouting have gone on down to the salon as we follow them. They must have found the wrecked generators. Maybe the helicopter too. I see a fire extinguisher on the wall and yank it off. Not quite as effective as a Magnum but it could come in handy.

Arnaud kicks the door open. Bertolini and his crew of four are at the windows, firing out into the night. I see Baldy and Driver among them. As they turn towards us, I let off the fire extinguisher and a huge whoosh of foam blasts across at them. Baldy drops his gun and yells as the foam hits his eyes. The other three turn their guns on us until the foam gets to their eyes too. They don't like it any more than Baldy, and it doesn't do a lot for their aim.

A shot goes close by my head. At the same time, I see Arnaud take a flying karate leap at Bertolini and kick the gun out of his hands. It goes off and blows a hole in the wall. Bertolini pulls a knife. The slim blade gleams in the half light from the emergency lamps.

The other four men are still yelling and trying to wipe the foam from their eyes. I give them another long blast as Michel jumps in through the window like a panther. He lands a massive kick in Bertolini's back as he goes for Arnaud. Bertolini staggers but gets his footing again. Arnaud kicks at the hand that's holding the knife but misses this time. Michel grabs Bertolini round the neck and gets thrown off like he's a child.

Then Bertolini and Arnaud are circling slowly in the

middle of the room. Bertolini's still holding the knife. I can hear Arnaud gasping for breath as he tries to draw on energy reserves he hasn't got.

Out of the corner of my eye, I see Baldy struggle to his feet and reach for his gun. Before he can get near it, Michel grabs him. He drags him towards the open window. Lenny's waiting there. His hands close round Baldy's neck. The scar below his eye is red and angry. 'For my brother!' For a moment, I think he's going to tip his captive out over the ledge. Instead, he gives him a punch in the head that isn't going to give Baldy any sweet dreams tonight.

The thickset figure of Bertolini, shadowy in the dim light, moves in on Arnaud, the slim stiletto in his hand. I'm powerless to help. I still have these three dudes I have to keep blasting with the fire extinguisher.

Michel stamps on the hand of one of them then kicks him in the jaw as he crawls towards a gun. Another is trying to get up, wiping foam out of his eyes, when Becks rushes forward with one of her screwdrivers. 'Bad idea!' She holds it at his throat. He sits.

Driver is fumbling inside his jacket – for a gun, a knife? I give him another jet right in his face but not so powerful. The extinguisher's running out. I think, This is all we need, but it isn't, because then I see a shadow in the open door of the salon. So we got the numbers wrong, there's another of them come to the party. I glance at Michel but he's busy with the dude whose jaw he's just broken. Lenny is tensed, ready to go for Driver, when four things happen almost at once.

Bertolini's hand flicks, the knife flashes towards

Arnaud and there's a single gunshot. The knife rattles away across the room.

I see a look of sheer terror on the faces of Bertolini's crew, astonishment on his and utter wonder on Arnaud's. It looks like Monsieur, standing there motionless, holding the gun. He's just a dark silhouette in the light from the corridor, but the dim lights gleam on short cropped silver hair. There's no mistaking his quiet, iron-cold voice. 'Still picking on youngsters, Alfredo? You should know better by now.'

As Bertolini lunges towards him, Monsieur points the gun directly at the Corsican's head and says softly, 'I wouldn't, if I were you.'

Bertolini's rasping voice is mocking. 'You really want this son who hates you so much? He would kill you as soon as look at you. He would kill you now, wouldn't you, Arnaud caro mio?'

Arnaud looks at his father. His face is empty of all expression, except traces of the wonder that I saw when Monsieur's silhouette appeared in the doorway. Then, he looks slowly back at Bertolini. He's shuddering for breath, his face trickling with sweat. The delirium of the withdrawal symptoms has caught up with him again; all his strength is gone. The room is completely quiet. No one moves a muscle. We're all of us watching like we're hypnotised.

Monsieur never takes his eyes off Bertolini. But there's some kind of exchange going on there between him and Arnaud. Like when I phoned Becks and she could read my mind about what I desperately wanted her to say to help me escape from my prison in that blue glass office.

Bertolini isn't finished yet. 'You can't win up here with just a bunch of crazy kids, you fool. And this time, no coming back from the dead when we're done with you. That's my gun in your hand. You just fired the last bullet in the chamber.'

Monsieur's expression never changes. Still pointing the gun, he fixes Bertolini's eyes with his own like he's on radar lock. 'You should learn to count as well as shoot straight, Alfredo.'

I hold my breath at this deadly game of bluff and double bluff. Then Becks shouts, 'Driver's got a knife!'

Lenny's across the room like a dancing boxer. He grabs Driver's head and the dude next to him. CRACK! He bangs their heads together so hard, we can hear bone against bone. They slump forward, out for the count. The same second, with a savage fury, Monsieur smashes the butt of his gun onto Bertolini's head. The Corsican goes down like a falling bull. And I think, So Monsieur knew all the time he had no bullets left after the one he used to save Arnaud from Bertolini's knife. How cool is that?

CHAPTER 11

Tunnel Vision

Only one of Bertolini's gang is still awake. Looking nervously at Lenny he raises his hands, all the fight knocked out of him.

Monsieur surveys the inert bodies. 'Hurry, tie them up before they come round!' The ropes they used when Becks and I first visited are coiled casually on the bar. Lenny and Michel grab Bertolini's unconscious body and lash his hands behind his back. Becks and I get to work on the others. In a few minutes, all five of our bad men are tied tightly to the ceiling pillars.

I look at my watch. Half five. The sky glows gold and blue behind the mountains. Arnaud is sat down, looking exhausted, talking in a low voice with his father. We pick up the knives and guns from the floor and throw them out of the window over the cliff.

As the last gun flies out of sight Monsieur says, 'Now we must depart from this place, and quickly.'

I'm puzzled by the urgency in his voice. We pick up our torches, and brace ourselves for the long climb down the stairs and back into the tunnel. Before we leave the room, Monsieur takes a last glance back at the heavy form of Bertolini slumped, still unconscious, roped firmly to the pillar.

'He won't get out of that, Monsieur.'

'He will try very hard, Joe.'

'So would I if I was in his shoes, with police on the way.'

Monsieur's grey eyes look at the mountains, as the dawn starts to flood the craggy slopes with light. 'It is not the police that he fears the most.' He turns towards the stairs. 'Come … '. As I follow Monsieur, I chew over his remark all the way down the steps to the tunnel. It takes my mind off my aching legs. By the time we go into the tunnel, I've decided that Bertolini must be afraid of bears paying him a visit through that open window. Perhaps Baldy didn't meet that bear in the woods. Maybe it turned up for breakfast like a reverse of the Goldilocks story.

'You're quiet.' Becks slips her hand into mine as we tramp along following the flashing torchlight.

'I was thinking about bears.'

'What, here?'

'Not coming after us. Just bears in the mountains.'

'I think he was making it up, it was the brandy …'

Lenny hisses behind us, 'Train!' We jump and he laughs.

'That is SO not funny, Lenny!'

'Sorry, Becks. You guys going home now? Or you got plans?' Lenny must be feeling really good. This is the longest speech I've ever heard from him.

'Well I'm going home, for definite. I'm going to live in the shower for a week, coming out only for chocolate at regular intervals.'

'What 'bout you, Joe?'

'I've got plans, me. A month of non-stop Top Gear with a plate of bacon, eggs, beans and chips that automatically refills every fifteen minutes. Oh, and there'll be a Coke tanker outside with a tube that goes straight into my glass.'

Becks looks back at Michel. 'Et toi, Michel? Tu vas retourner à la Camargue?'

He laughs shyly. 'À la Camargue, oui. Ça me manque.'

Those three simple words, 'I miss it', make my eyes suddenly sting. I'd give anything just to be sat in our kitchen again with Jack's band blasting the tiles off the roof, Mum cooking up coq au vin and Grandad setting the table while he looks for his glasses.

'How about you, Lenny?'

'Interview. Tuesday.'

My brain does a somersault and crashes as I ask it a question. I turn to Becks. 'What day of the week is it?'

She consults her mobile. 'Sunday. That is so weird. I was sure today was Monday.'

'What's the interview for, Lenny?'

'Gym, Stroud. Trainee fitness instructor.'

So Lenny was ready to let a job interview go to come out here for his brother and his mate, not knowing when or even if he'd ever get home. My face burns. Then another thought crosses my mind. Sunday. The eighth day. If we can get a flight from Marseille tonight, I'll be home when I promised. Just. But the mission's not quite over yet. I drop back to walk next to Monsieur and Arnaud.

'When can I call DI Wellington, Monsieur?'

'After we have disembarked at Marseille, you call him, Joe.'

I desperately want to ask Monsieur about Dad but it doesn't seem the right time, when he's only just been reunited with his son. Then another thought strikes me about what could scare Bertolini more than the police, and it hits me so hard that all the way back down the mountain, I can't think of anything else.

I do remember to listen out for hissing rails. But perhaps the train's got well stuck on the slopes this time because there's not a horn blast to be heard.

Then Becks shouts, 'I can see it!'

'The train?'

'No, duh! The end of the tunnel!'

It's just a pinprick of light at first but it slowly gets bigger. Forty minutes later we're blinking in the bright sunlight. Vivario station is still as eerily deserted as it was last night. There are no guards to spot us as we clamber off the rails and onto the platform. Becks looks at the worn notice board. 'What time is it?'

'Half eight.'

'Two minutes for the train to Calvi.'

'Lucky or what?'

Her eyes widen as it dawns on her. 'Oh-my-God ...'

—⚮—

An hour and a half later we're on the ferry, heading for the restaurant and almost dribbling at the thought of steak and chips.

'It is safer if we eat at tables that are at a distance from

149

each other. You, Joe, go with Becks and Arnaud. I will go with Lenny and Michel. We watch out for each other, OK?'

'OK.' The question's burning in my brain. 'Monsieur … how did you …?'

'When you have eaten, I will be on deck. We can talk, then.'

As Becks and I tuck into our steaks, it's good to see Arnaud making short work of his. 'How're you feeling, Arnaud?'

He looks across to the table on the far side of the restaurant, where Monsieur is eating and talking with Lenny and Michel. Then he looks back at us and just nods, with the half smile of his dad.

Remembering Monsieur's warning, I take a quick glance round at the families with tired children, picking at their chips.

Becks whispers, 'What do you think of Ant and Dec?'

'What …?'

'Dudes at the table next door.'

I sneak a look. The two men are dark haired and black suited; their skin is pale, like they don't get to see daylight that often. They sit silently, scowling over their coffees.

'Dates didn't show?'

'Mais qu'est-ce que tu fais?' Our creatures of the night turn to watch the commotion at the table next to them, where a small kid is being impressively sick all over his chips and his dad, and being shouted at by his mum.

I whisper to Becks and Arnaud, 'D'you think dad

could be undercover police and this is some kind of diversion?'

Arnaud shrugs and grins. 'He just looks like a dad with sick on his trousers.'

Dad yells at small boy and wife, who is grabbing at serviettes, 'Mais qu'est-ce que je peux faire, moi?' He stomps off to the Men's, while his wife mops up and carries on scolding small kid on his behalf.

Out of the corner of my eye, I notice that the Undead have now turned their attention to us. I exchange glances with Becks and Arnaud. Becks peruses the menu. 'They do choc mousse. Who's up for pud?'

'I could handle that. So long as comes in a lake of choc sauce. Arnaud?'

'Not chocolate mousse, no.' He scans the menu. 'I think, the vanilla ice cream, with an OCEAN of chocolate sauce.' He pauses then says deliberately with a mischievous smile, 'I just love the way the chocolate sauce oozes down the ice cream.'

There's an abrupt scrape of chairs as our neighbours get up quickly, faces an even whiter shade of pale, and almost run out of the restaurant. Becks has to bury her face in her serviette to hide her snorts of laughter. Arnaud and I are still grinning as we join the queue for desserts.

—◆—

When I find him, Monsieur is looking out over the sea at the shrinking island of Corsica. The air is warm, the sun beating down as we sail away from the mountains that sink slowly towards the horizon. I lean on the rail next to him. Maybe one day, Becks and I will go back and camp on those mountains to gaze at the shooting stars; but not until all the bad men are locked up.

I look at Monsieur closely for the first time in a while. The blood is gone from his forehead and there's a vivid red scar instead. He's thinner but he also looks years younger. There's a light in his eyes that I've never seen before.

He turns to me. 'You're wondering what on earth happened after you found me in that room – yes?'

I nod. He says slowly, 'There is a link between body and mind that the Guardiens know well. It is called in French 'la kinésthésie'. Kinaesthesia is a technique whereby the mind learns consciously to control the vital organs, muscles and blood circulation. To use kinaesthesia, you have to be able first of all to put yourself into a state of total relaxation, where you descend 'au bord du sommeil' – to the edge of sleep. The technique is used as a physical and mental therapy in many more enlightened parts of France.'

He looks out again across the blue sea. 'What is not commonly known or practised is beyond 'le bord du sommeil'. It is a state that is like a little brother to death itself. You take yourself down to another level. Your pulse drops to almost nil. The blood retreats from your veins to the vital organs, so your skin looks like you are dead. Your heart almost stops; it slows to such a rate that you have no pulse that can be felt. The Guardiens have had to do this when the Mistral is blowing so cold that no one could survive otherwise.'

'So is it like going into a human kind of hibernation, Monsieur?'

'Exactly that, Joe. And that is how you found me.'

'So when they fired on us as we left Les Baux …?'

'I was expecting them, on the way up there and all the way back down.'

'When the gun went off, you came off Mistral to make them think they'd hit you, so we could escape with Arnaud?'

'The bullet went wide. I hit my head, probably on a rock, when I fell. The gash served its purpose. They concluded after a few fairly crude attempts to check if I was still alive, that the fall had killed me. That must have been a great disappointment to Bertolini. I'm sure he was looking forward to making my death far more drawn out.'

I remember what might have been the slight movement of his hand in the flickering candle light, as we left that awful room. 'What was it that brought you back, Monsieur?'

'The first sense you have, long before you are born, is hearing. It is also the last sense to leave you when you depart from this life. From the very sea floor of that dead sleep, I heard Arnaud's voice.'

The mountains of Corsica have disappeared below the horizon. Monsieur is gazing at the waves, back with his own thoughts. It's not the right time to ask that other nagging question. I slip quietly away.

—◊◊◊—

'Joe! How are you? WHERE are you?'

'Marseille. There isn't a lot of time, Inspector …'

'Your mum called yesterday. Said you and Rebecca had left the French family and gone off to help out some mates, God knows where, and they haven't heard from you since.'

'We did go to help out some mates. We're on our way home now. But …'

'She was seriously worried, Joe. What exactly have you two been up to?'

'I would've called but there wasn't a signal, Inspector, and …'

'There are still those old-fashioned devices called land lines, Joe.'

'Not where we were.'

He exhales loudly into the phone. 'So just where were you?'

'Corsica. Tying up Bertolini and his crew like parcels as a present for you, Inspector.'

'BERTOLINI! What on EARTH …?'

'You'd better be quick, Inspector. Or the bears might get to him before you do.'

'Bears? What are you …?'

'Can you call me back? I'm almost out of credit.'

'Don't move, Joe!'

'Before you call me, Inspector, can you give a message to my grandad? Please?'

'Of course I'll give him a message. What is it?'

'Tell him the mates are OK. And I've kept my promise.'

—⁓—

'Aurevoir Joe, Becks.' Michel hugs us then turns to Lenny. 'Tu es un bon copain!' He and Lenny exchange a high five.

'You too. Good partner, Michel. Come visit anytime.'

'Viens visiter la Camargue, Lenny.'

Lenny nods, a slow smile breaking out. 'Might do, Michel …'

'Vas bien, mon frère. À la prochaine fois!' Arnaud and Michel really could be brothers as they make their farewells. Like they know they'll see each other again sometime. It makes me feel quite envious.

'À la prochaine, Arnaud!' With a light step, Michel strides away towards his train and the homeland he's longing to see again.

'Lenny, your train goes in five minutes! Don't want to miss that interview, do you?' Becks is almost hopping from one foot to another. 'Good luck with it, Lenny! Will you teach me kick boxing when you land the job?'

'For sure.'

'Catch you in Stroud soon, mate.'

'Yeah. Soon. See you. Joe. Becks.'

He turns awkwardly to Monsieur and Arnaud. 'See you dudes, sometime …'

He's caught up in a massive, back-slapping hug from Arnaud. 'You have been a mighty ally to me and my father, Lenny. We will never forget that.'

'Cool. See you, then …'

He melts into the night, heading towards the station, among the crowds thronging Marseille ferry port.

Monsieur turns to us, that new light gleaming in his grey eyes. His voice is even quieter than usual. 'My dear friends. You have given me back my son and my life.'

I mess up an attempt at a French shrug, and go for an English grin instead. 'It's never boring around you, Monsieur.'

Becks says, 'Are you going home now, Monsieur?'

His voice is gentle, like he's giving a child some bad news but trying to make it sound not so bad. 'We cannot return to the chateau just yet, Becks. Unfortunately, the police will be looking for me more diligently than ever, once Bertolini is arrested.'

'Not when we tell them that he tried to kill you!'

Arnaud's voice is as quiet as Monsieur's. 'Becks, we know Bertolini well. He is an expert at twisting the truth. He will make every effort to implicate my father and me in the drug running, to save himself from the severest penalty.'

Becks looks shell-shocked. I don't feel that surprised but there's a leaden feeling in my stomach. 'So … what are you going to do? Where will you go?'

'We have friends who will give us shelter, Joe.'

'The Guardiens?'

'Among others. Once Arnaud is completely well again, I will see what can be done to clear his name and mine.'

'But you'll need our help. We're like, witnesses, aren't we? We SAW …!'

'What you saw, what you know, and what the police will believe, are not necessarily the same thing, Joe.'

How well I know that, after the hit and run that wasn't me; the random accident that brought me and Becks all this way. I stare at Monsieur, knowing that he's right but not wanting to. I'm so desperate to try and sort it all out. Then that nagging question that hit me in the tunnel bursts out of its box, bumps around my head and comes out of my mouth. 'Monsieur, up on the mountain, you said it wasn't the Corsican police that Bertolini fears the most. Did you mean Commander Julius Grayling?'

I see a flicker of surprise on Arnaud's face. Becks looks at me with the same expression. Monsieur's voice is gentle. 'Joe, it is a long time since I have heard from Commander Grayling. If it was in my power to bring you back together with the father you used to know, then dear God I would.'

'When you said that everything changed ...'

Monsieur takes a look round at the people rushing past us; this isn't the place or the time. But we both know there will never be a right place and a right time. Taking my arm, he gently steers me out of the crowd towards some benches and we sit down. As he talks, his voice is calm, but the pain in his eyes brings that night at the chateau back to me with such force, I can see the shadowy room with all its pictures. 'Joe, both your father and I, for different reasons, became part of the very evil we were fighting. I fear that, even if it was possible, any attempt to win your father back would almost certainly destroy you both.'

I stare at Monsieur's troubled eyes, and I know that he's trying to protect me from some knowledge that he has. But I feel like he's handed me a prison sentence. Around us, the busy concourse has turned into a blur.

He says softly, 'I am deeply sorry, Joe. This is a terrible thing for me to have to tell you. But for your own safety – and for your father's sake too – you must not try to find him.'

CHAPTER 12

Harm's Way

'What does Monsieur know about Dad that he won't tell me?' As the plane climbs into the night, I look out of the window and see the reflection of a tramp, with huge bags under his eyes.

Becks whispers, 'It could be that he can't tell you, Joe. If it's something that bad …'

'Well he should let me be the judge of that!'

'I think we have to trust Monsieur.'

'I'm not giving up on my dad, Becks! If Monsieur won't help me, I'll find someone else who can.'

'Keep your voice down!'

Cringing at the thought of how many people have overheard my outburst, I cast anxious glances around. Most passengers are either dozing or reading. I can't see who's sat behind us, but I sure as anything can smell something that's nothing to do with the coffee, tea and biscuits that are going round. 'Have you put some perfume on?'

'Oh yeah, like I carry a tank of Chanel Number Five around with me …' Becks sniffs. 'Actually, I can smell something. P'raps they've scented the plane's air con. It's pretty awful … too sweet and heavy.'

We look closely at the air hostess who puts trays of coffee and biscuits in front of us. Then we take another sniff as she moves on up the aisle.

'Now that IS Chanel Number Five.' Becks sips her coffee, then wrinkles her nose. 'You can have this, it's too strong for me.'

'D'you want my biscuits? I don't do choc chip.'

We jump as there's a quiet swish like a hissing snake, from the seat right behind us. A woman glides past. All we can see is her back. She's in a dark blue, satiny dress, with one of these shawl things draped round her shoulders. Her bleach-blonde hair is pulled so tightly up on her head that it looks painful. She walks with a confident, fashion model swing.

Becks watches her as she goes up to the air hostess. 'Classy pashmina, if you like that sort of thing. Shame about the ...'

I wonder what she was going to say because Becks doesn't normally do catty. Then, my nose catches the waft of air following the shawl. It's that same sweet, cloying scent. The woman turns and comes back down the aisle towards us, a small bottle of tonic water in her hand.

Becks whispers, 'I've seen her before ...'

The woman's face is like the ones in glossy magazines. It's perfectly made up. The skin is stretched tight across the cheek bones. Carefully defined, pale blue eyes survey us beneath arching eyebrows. Her dress rustles as she approaches and stops by our seat. She flashes us a smile that shows a set of gleaming, too-perfect white teeth. The smile doesn't get to her eyes. Her voice is slightly husky, like she's a smoker. 'I hope you won't think me intrusive but aren't you the youngsters who were pulled off the Bristol Gorge in that amazing rescue?'

She rests a hand on the seat in front of us. Diamonds glitter on her ring finger. On her little finger there's a gold signet ring. Staring, mesmerised, I can just make out some letters, engraved in an elaborate script. 'Yeah, well, feels like a long time ago now.'

Becks takes a loud, crunching bite on one of my choc chip cookies.

'You were both so brave! I was watching it on the TV and my heart was in my mouth as you climbed up that awful cliff.' She pauses, pale blue eyes homing in on me like headlights. 'Do tell me, how did you come to be there?'

Becks has a sudden fit of coughing. Bits of cookie fly everywhere. The diamonds retreat as Pashmina flicks her hand out of range. My brain thrashes wildly around in the few seconds segway. 'It … was a crazy idea. Like, a bet with some mates that went wrong.'

Pashmina laughs, a low, throaty sound. 'You young people! You are so reckless. My daughter is the same. I can never dare let her out of my sight.'

I glance at the seat behind us but I can't see any daughter under surveillance. The headlights switch to main beam and the eyebrows crinkle slightly. The husky voice is still teasing but there's an edge to it now. 'And are you two returning home from another great adventure? Another bet, perhaps?'

Becks' foot clamps mine to the floor as she says

brightly, 'I've seen you before, haven't I? Weren't you in Yah! magazine last month?'

Pashmina ignores her, fixing me with those pale blue headlights. 'Was the great adventure by any chance in Corsica?'

I almost yelp as the pressure on my foot intensifies.

'Got it! You won the Yah! award for the most unusual cosmetic intervention, didn't you? Is your name Chantelle? Or, was it Chantal?'

People turn from their seats and look at us. Pashmina darts a venomous glance at Becks and gives me a shuddering smile. She slides back into her seat. I can feel her eyes boring into the back of my head.

I whisper, 'Becks – my foot, please?'

'Don't talk to prying strangers, then!'

'What did you mean about seeing her before?'

Her whisper is as quiet as mine. 'The cafe, in Aix. Just before Bertolini turned up. Those pale blue eyes. The cream leather jacket. Remember?'

'I remember you saying. But I never saw her.'

'Then you'll just have to believe me.'

'I do believe you. And I don't like her any more than you do.'

For the rest of the flight, that sickly perfume reminds us who's sitting behind. As we join the queue for the exit, I keep an uneasy eye open for the shawl. It's nowhere to be seen. We stagger out of the arrivals lounge on stiff legs and look around for Grandad's car. In those few brief seconds while I try to orientate myself, a voice hisses in my ear, 'How like Julius you are, my dear. He would be very proud …'

For a moment, I can't register what I've heard. I only know that the voice is hers and she's using my dad's first name like she knows him. Then everything melts together and it all goes off like a chemical explosion in my brain. I whirl round, to see Becks pointing towards flashing blue lights. DI Wellington waves us impatiently into a squad car.

'Are you taking us to the station, Inspector?'

'We'll want you both there tomorrow, Joe. Or rather, at a more civilised hour, later on today. But right now, we're taking you both to your homes.'

'My grandad …'

'Both your families know. Just a sensible precaution.'

Becks says, 'Have you got Bertolini?'

'The French police have him, and the rest of them.'

I say, with a sudden sense of alarm, 'The rest of them?'

He turns to look at us, sat in the passenger seat behind him. 'The five men who were found tied up in the house at Vivario are in custody. Are you saying there were more of them, Joe?'

The driver brakes hard and hits the horn as a lorry carves us up.

'No. You've got all your bad men, Inspector.'

'I'll send a car for you at five, Joe. We'll collect you at ten past, Rebecca.'

Becks doesn't even twitch at being Rebecca'd again. She looks out of the window at the flashing lights of a plane flying low over us as it comes in to land. She seems lonely, somehow; as though I'm not here beside her. And I realise that part of me hasn't left the airport.

I'm still hearing that voice and the words it hissed into my ear. For the first time, I wonder if I should do what Becks wants me to: trust Monsieur, go home and live my life. 'You alright, Becks?'

'Mmm.'

'Something on your mind?'

She shakes her head. I'm sure it isn't really a No, but I can't ask her. There are just too many listening ears around us again. I reach out my hand and grab hers. It feels cold. 'We've got to stick together, Becks. We'll be alright if we do that.' Then and there, I decide to stop troubling Becks about my dad and all the darkness that seems to go with him.

The squad car drops Becks off first. I walk with her to the door. Steve opens it, holding a can of lager. Top Gear is going at full throttle in their lounge. He grins at the car. 'What have you two been up to now?'

'Leave it, big bro.' Becks' voice is dead tired.

'Driven any exotic cars lately, Joe?'

'Not cars, no. See y'later, Becks.' She looks pale in the light from the hall. I give her a hug. 'We'll do a film or something, after ...'

'Night, Joe.' She turns and wanders into the house. As I get back into the car, I know it's that Pashmina woman with her stinking scent and nosey questions that must be worrying her.

As we pull up outside my house there's a light on in the lounge. I remember the last time a cop car took me home after that chase down the M5. The neighbours must think they've got a juvenile defender, or whatever it is, living next door.

'Five pm, Joe. It'll give you the chance for a good lie-in. Make sure you're ready.'

'I'll be ready, Inspector.' The squad car moves quietly off.

The front door's ajar, a glow of light behind it. Suddenly, that dream I had about Becks flying like Wendy comes back to me. I stare at the door, as I remember the story. About Peter Pan's mother not leaving the window open anymore, so he couldn't come home. And another boy was in his bed.

Grandad opens the door wide, the light glinting on his glasses. They're on the top of his head. 'Joe?' He blinks out at me.

'Hi, Grandad.'

'Well, don't just stand there. I've brewed up a pot of tea.'

He puts a welcoming arm round my shoulders as we go into the lounge. I look at the worn sofa and the photos of me and Jack on the mantelpiece. There's one of me winning the egg and spoon race, aged five. It used to make me cringe.

'Where's Mum?'

He pours two mugs of tea. 'She went to bed a couple of hours ago.'

'Is she alright? I mean …'

He takes his mug, hands the other one to me, and sits down in his usual armchair. 'She's alright. We … had a bit of a chat that night, after you called. Biscuit?'

'They gave us loads on the plane, thanks.' I take a swig of tea. 'What did you chat about?'

'Nothing lofty, about giving children their independence and all that sort of twaddle. I ... told your mother a little story.' He clears his throat, and takes a mouthful of tea.

'What was the story about?'

'Myself, as it happens. It was you who reminded me, Joe.'

I put my mug down. 'About having to help out a mate and not being able to tell anyone? You told me it happened to you too.'

'Only once.' He smiles. 'Not like you! But I was about your age.' He takes a choc chip biscuit and looks at it thoughtfully. 'They're so bad for the waistline once you hit sixty.'

'Are you going to tell me? I mean, you don't have to ... but ...'

'I'd like to tell you, Joe.' He puts the biscuit down and leans back in his armchair. 'Nik Wasilek was a new pupil in our class. Polish. Very bright. He was staying with an English family while his parents saved up the money to come over here too. We became friends. My parents even invited him to tea. Very charitable of them, they must have thought. Like so many of their generation, they had a distrust of foreigners.'

'But you don't. The Gautiers ...?'

'I didn't share my parents' values, Joe, although I still loved them. It was easier to keep quiet. One day, Nik came up to me after school. He looked very frightened. He said that the father was drinking and having terrible

165

rows with the mother. Then, they would turn on him, as though it was all his fault. He'd phoned his father. Asked him to take him away. But it would be two days before his dad could come over for him.'

'What did you do?'

'I hid Nik in my room. What else could I do?'

I stare at Grandad.

'Of course, it wasn't easy. I had to tell no end of lies to my parents. Smuggling food up and all that. I became very inventive.'

'Didn't the family contact the police? They could have come round and searched.'

'I was banking on the probability that they wouldn't welcome a police investigation, having treated Nik the way they did.'

'And … did his dad come for him?'

He picks up his mug and takes a swallow. 'That was the trickiest bit. Nik's dad was waiting in a taxi, just up the road. My parents were both in the lounge. I had to get them out of the house or they'd see us coming down the stairs.'

'So …?'

'There weren't mobile phones then. But there was an extension land-line in my parents' bedroom. I called the fire brigade. Told them our next door neighbour's chimney was on fire. Everyone had coal fires in those days.'

'So the fire engine comes blaring down the road …'

'And my parents rushed outside to get a look, just like the rest of the street. Nik and I nipped out the back door. It worked a treat.'

'Didn't you get into awful trouble?'

Grandad drains his mug of tea. 'The police couldn't trace phone calls at that time.' He glances at his watch. 'Dear God, it's late.'

My tea's gone cold. 'What did Mum say – when you told her?'

'She asked me what on earth that had to do with you going off for eight days in France without telling us why.'

'Is she still …?'

He gets up, and puts the mugs on the tray. 'Your mother worries, Joe – it's perfectly understandable. Now, get to bed. It's good to have you back.'

'It's good to be home, Grandad.'

He pats my arm as I head for the stairs then pauses, his hand on the light switch. 'Perhaps we'll hear the story of your latest adventure one day, Joe. When you're ready?'

'You will, Grandad. And … thanks.'

'Sleep well, Joe. Take care.' He switches on the landing light and I drag my aching legs slowly upstairs.

As I slip into my bed, Fats slides reluctantly off my pillow and wraps himself warmly round my feet. My eyes closing, I think, 'I had no idea Grandad was so cool.'

In the early hours of the morning there's a roaring storm, and I wake up while it's still dark to hear the wind lashing round my window. But Fats creeps back onto my pillow, and his massive purring drowns all the noise of the wind and rain.

CHAPTER 13

Never Forget Me

'Want that last bit of lasagne, Joe? I can manage without, honest.'

'I'm stuffed. You have it, bud.'

'What does the Inspector want to talk to you about, Joe?' Mum's voice is carefully casual as she scrapes the lasagne onto Jack's plate. It's the first question she's asked me about where I've been for those missing days. I've no idea what Grandad's told her.

'The guys we went to help out had some bad men after them. But they've all been arrested now.'

'So he just wants witness statements?'

'That's all he wants, Mum.'

'And that's why you came home in a police car?'

'DI Wellington said it was a sensible precaution.'

She runs hot water into the oven dish. 'I'm glad he thought so.'

Jack whispers, 'Did they have shooters?'

DRING! Saved by the doorbell. 'That'll be the car.'

Mum dries her hands on a tea towel. 'Would you like me to pick you and Becks up after the interview?'

'Thanks, but it's OK. We'll maybe take in a film then get the train.'

She reaches for her handbag. 'Your Grandad said you might.'

'Mum, it's alright, I still have money left after the trip.'

'Then you must have been living off thin air!'

'One of the mates gave us some dosh …' I just daren't say how much.

'Don't be back later than ten, Joe.'

—∞—

Becks' hair is back to its old self, swishing around in a red cloud as she slips into the back seat beside me. She looks a lot brighter.

'How was hair wash, Becks?'

'I died and went to heaven.'

'And the chocolate?'

'All chocked out. Want a Revel?'

'Thanks.'

I look at the driver. He doesn't seem to be wired for sound but you never know. I whisper, 'What do you think DIW's going to ask us?'

'Just about everything, I s'pose.'

'We can miss out Lenny and Michel, can't we? They'd hate to get dragged into police interviews.'

She looks at me and shakes her head. 'We can't miss anything out. If we do, and it gets picked up, DIW will never believe another word we say. He'll carry on thinking that Monsieur's a drugs baron.'

'What makes you think he'll believe a word we say anyway?'

'The parcels we left for him on the mountain, that's what.'

'Have you been talking to someone about it?'

'Yeah. Myself. I had a long time in the shower to think it through.'

Detective Inspector Wellington's got someone else with him as we sit down again in that interview room. The room is as bleak as ever, with bars on the windows and no carpets on the concrete floor. DIW's mate is a young dude with floppy hair, wearing thick, black-rimmed glasses and a creased suit. He smiles at us in a friendly way. He doesn't look like a cop at all; more like a clever student who goes to lectures instead of parties.

'Meet Archie, my second-in-command. He's going to be doing the computer stuff because frankly, I hate the things.'

The Boffin shakes our hands. 'Thanks for coming in, guys. You must be tired after all the travel.'

DIW sits down heavily in the chair opposite us. 'Tea, coffee?' He looks worn out. I wonder what kind of life he has when he's not chasing bad men.

'Thanks, but we're OK, Inspector.'

Boff opens up the grimy laptop that we saw last time we were here, and logs in. DIW looks at me. 'A journalist, Miss Charlotte Wickham, came to us with a recording of a conversation, Joe. Do you know her?'

I'm back in St Mary Redcliffe, Driver right next to me. 'I didn't know her, Inspector. But she did contact me.'

'One of the voices on the recording sounds like yours. The conversation appears to be a deal of some kind and it gave us abundant cause for concern. You were going back to Bertolini in return for an awful lot of money? Was that the deal?'

My face feels hot. 'It wasn't the money. I just wanted to make them believe that it was. I thought I could help Monsieur because he had nothing to do with the drug running.'

DIW's bushy dark eyebrows are frowning. 'Shortly afterwards, you and Rebecca disappeared off the radar. We had surveillance at all the airports and ferry ports but turned up nothing.'

'They grabbed us at Temple Meads, knocked us out with some kind of jab and took us to Corsica in a helicopter, Inspector. There was no passport control on that route.' Becks' voice has the tiniest trace of irritation.

Still frowning, DIW switches on the recorder. 'Let's begin after I last saw you two. What were you doing in France?'

Telling the truth, the whole truth and nothing but the truth takes two grindingly long hours. My brain and my backside are aching and I think Boff is going to break that laptop, he's typing so fast.

As Becks and I put the whole story back together, I watch DIW's face. Wondering if he's finally going to believe us about Monsieur. He exchanges looks with his F1 typist when we tell them about Vivario. But he never interrupts, not once, until we get to Marseille. 'Was that the last you saw of Monsieur and his son?'

'We said goodbye to them at the ferry port. Then we took a cab to Marseille Marignane and got the plane.'

He asks, kind of casually, 'Was it an uneventful flight? Nothing unusual happened?'

I really don't want to tell DIW about Pashmina. I want to think it was just some random encounter with a weirdo on a plane. But Becks' foot nudges mine. 'There was this woman, sat behind us … she said she recognised us from when we were pulled off the Gorge.'

DIW leans forward and Boff's thundering fingers are going to blow up that keyboard. 'What else did she say, Joe?'

'She asked … if we were on our way back from Corsica.'

'Could she have overheard you talking together about where you'd been?'

'I know we didn't mention Corsica.'

'Can you describe her?'

Becks creates an image so vivid, I half expect to see Pashmina slide in through the door. DIW switches off the tape. 'I think we've all earned a coffee now. Save the file, Archie. I want the next bit to be off the record.'

Becks and I get up and walk around to stretch stiff legs as coffee and choc biscuits arrive. We glance at each other. Her eyes are approving. No foot clamping, so far.

DIW gives us a chance to get some of the coffee and biscuits inside then he turns to me. 'I want you to think back to your chauffeuring days, Joe. During your time at L'Étoile Fine Wines, did anyone say anything about an attempt to break into their computer system?'

My brain is on Fast Rewind, images from that night flashing past. 'The day after I did that last run to London, and found out what was in the boot, Madame de L'Étang said they'd had some kind of security scare. She said that was why no one was leaving the building.'

'Did she say what the security scare was?'

I can see a massive hole opening up in front of Monsieur if I tell the truth now. 'No, but Bertolini did. Just before he sent me on the run to Birmingham to collect Leah Wilks, he said that a rival organisation was trying to hack into their network.'

'Another drugs cartel?'

'I don't know. But those were the words.' Those were the words. Except that they were Monsieur's. But I'm never going to tell DIW that. Becks sits quietly, no fireworks and no footwork. She knows what the result would be if I don't tell this one lie for Monsieur.

DIW continues, 'There's been a build up of some kind of gang warfare over the last few months. Two shootings in Birmingham and a fatal one here in Bristol. We have reason to believe that both incidents were linked to drugs cartels; one of them, Bertolini's, the other, far less well known to us.'

'And now that Bertolini's out of the way …?'

'Exactly, Joe. The new boys on the block could have seen their chance, with boss man removed for some time to come.'

Becks and I exchange a quick look. DIW's talking about Bertolini as boss man – no mention of Monsieur.

'How much do you know about the new boys, Inspector?'

'Very little so far. A lot of it's hearsay, picked up by our undercover people. But we're pretty sure of two things –

the boss is a woman and she has quite a reputation in the underworld.'

Becks asks, 'What kind of reputation?'

'She doesn't shoot people who get in her way. That's not her style. She poisons them.'

The blunt words send a chill through my blood. Becks stares at DIW with a horrified fascination as he says grimly, 'She's very clever. Not your Agatha Christie arsenic in tea cups with finger prints all over them. There's never a shred of forensic evidence to point her way.'

'Then, what makes you think she poisons people?'

'When the victims are autopsied there are no signs of violence. Just a catastrophic organ failure; heart, liver or such like. But in an otherwise perfectly fit body, as though it's death from natural causes.'

Becks whispers, 'Couldn't it have been natural causes? I mean, it's awful, but it does happen, doesn't it?'

Boff says quietly, 'More detailed investigations revealed minute traces of chemical combinations that could trigger a fatal allergic reaction. The chemicals are so sophisticated that they must have been put together in a laboratory.'

'But why is this woman the suspect?'

Detective Inspector Wellington speaks slowly now. 'In every case we can trace a connection that the victim had with her. Sometimes very recent, sometimes many years back. But there's always a link.'

I watch Boff, as he clicks on folders in the laptop. 'Have you found something on the memory stick?'

He nods. 'Our hackers finally managed to crack

open a file that's been a real headache. Looks like a saved email. It's a photo, with three groups of letters beneath it. They could be initials, or perhaps some kind of code.'

A huge directory of files fills the screen. Suddenly, I'm back in that cave room with Becks, smoke in our throats and her fingers going Click, Double Click on the mouse. There's maybe a hundred files, all with coded names, letters jumbled up with numbers, like the ones we saw that night. But one file sticks out from the rest; it has an odd tag.

Becks says, 'That one? 'Unknown54. Retrieve and Discover'?'

Boff takes off his glasses as he looks at it. 'The name our hackers gave it, once they'd worked their magic. We've run the image through the database but no match.' He double clicks to open the file. Those cold blue eyes look straight at us.

DIW's voice is grave. 'Is this the woman on the plane, Joe?'

I stare at Pashmina's frozen face. And I remember Becks and I chatting away only inches in front of her. 'Yes.'

'Can you confirm that, Rebecca?'

'The hair was differently styled, but it's her alright.' She almost glares at DIW. 'So, you think this woman could be the one who poisons people. She's the boss of the cartel that's having a go at Bertolini's operation? Why, Inspector?'

'Because her appearance fits with descriptions our undercover people have given us. And because of where this file comes from. It's quite possible that Bertolini is well aware of her and what her mob is planning. We'll be interrogating him about this, of course. But he's unlikely to be very forthcoming. It would just add to the mountain of evidence against him.'

Mountain. Bears. What Monsieur said scared Bertolini more than the police. If it wasn't Commander Julius Grayling, did he mean this terrifying woman? My head swims as I see that hand with its two rings, clutching the seat on the plane.

DIW's sharp eyes are on me. 'Something ring a bell, Joe?'

Desperate not to drag Monsieur back into this, I stare at the three groups of letters beneath the photo:

PHSA   CR   NFM

'C R. She was wearing a gold signet ring with those letters.'

'A signet ring? So they could be initials. Database, Archie!' Boff does a quick exit.

DIW doesn't seem too happy, despite the new clue. He looks at us, long and hard. 'I'm concerned about this woman's interest in you two. I don't think she was on your plane by chance.'

Becks says, 'I saw her in Aix too, at the cafe. Just before Bertolini turned up.'

DIW's voice is as serious as I've ever heard it. 'There's a risk that the pair of you could get caught up again in all this. I'm going to give you a number that you must both put into your mobiles and code it, so you can call us fast if you need to.'

Just before we leave, a question that I was going to ask as I watched Boff on the laptop pops up again in my mind. 'What was the file called before the hackers renamed it, Inspector?'

He pauses. 'Good question, Joe. Archie'll know. I'll get back to you. Now, take care, both of you.'

On the way home in the squad car, Becks whispers, 'It's kind of ironic, isn't it? Bertolini's the only one who's safe from her right now, in his cosy little police cell. How did you notice that C R?'

'You were stuffing my choc chip cookies into your mouth at the time, then you coughed all over Pashmina.'

'I choked deliberately!'

'Which is why you didn't notice the ring.'

'So, whose could those initials be? If they are initials?'

'That's down to the police database now, isn't it?'

'Oh, come on, Joe! Databases are only as clever as the questions they're asked. They'll get zillions of C Rs.'

'They're bound to do more complex queries than just C R. But …'

'Share the idea, Sherlock!'

I'm not sure where this is going to lead us. 'We all of us kind of assumed that it was Bertolini who put the file there, didn't we? But Monsieur used that computer, too. And Monsieur is Le Comte de la Rochelle, isn't he? C for Comte, R for Rochelle.'

'More like M L C D L R!'

'There's only so much that you can get onto a signet ring that fits round your little finger, Becks.'

'OK, Mister Clever – but signet rings were originally used as seals, with wax, to prove that you'd written a letter, or signed a death warrant, or something.'

'So?'

'So you'd put your own initials on it. Not somebody else's.'

The driver indicates left to pull off the M5 at the Stroud junction. I'm still not sure where my brain is going. 'You would, if the ring was your own.'

'Are you saying … what ARE you saying?'

'Suppose Pashmina's ring actually belongs to Monsieur and she maybe stole it? Or perhaps she had the ring made for herself, with his initials.'

'Why would she … ? Oh, no, that's not possible! This horrible woman who poisons people and runs a drugs gang … you're saying she could somehow be connected with Monsieur?'

My brain is in full retreat now. But it's going in a new direction that I don't like any more than the last. 'You're right, it's not possible. Because she wouldn't have used the word 'Comte', she'd have used Monsieur's first name.'

'Which is … ?'

'I don't know. But it's all looking far too unlikely anyway, isn't it?'

As the car pulls up outside her house, Becks' voice is triumphant, 'I bet it's simply that her initials are C R, like we all thought in the first place.'

'I really hope it is that simple, Becks. Catch you at break tomorrow?'

'Grab me a tuna baguette, will you? Dad never has any dinner money for me.'

I go up to her front door with her as she takes out her key and unlocks. The house looks empty; no lights are on.

'Is your dad not home? Steve?'

'No idea.'

'D'you want to crash at our place? You could bring all your school stuff and go in on the bus with me and Jack?'

'I'll be alright. Anyway,' she yawns, 'I've got homework. And so have you.'

Watching her disappear into that dark house, I shout after her, 'I'll call you later, alright?'

—∞—

All the lights are off in my house too as the car drops me off. The cop driver turns to me. 'You got a key?'

'It's OK. The front door'll be open.'

'Your parents should give you a key, y'know. Bad idea, leaving the door open.'

'Thanks for the lift.'

He drives off. I lock the door behind me and tiptoe up the stairs. Creeping into my bedroom, I switch on the light and punch DIW's number into my mobile. Fats yowls outside my room. I stumble across to let him in before he wakes up the whole house.

DIW answers, the buzz of his office in the background. I wonder if he's been there all night. 'The original file name was meaningless, Joe. That's why our hackers changed it.'

'What was it, Inspector?'

'Just a jumble of letters and numbers.'

'Can you read them out to me?'

'Archie's emailing them to you as we speak. Now

look after yourselves. And call us if there's anything that worries you.'

Sat on my bed with the keyboard on my lap, I hit my email. There's two hundred and four unopened messages, most of them spam, the rest from mates. Looks like I've missed a load of parties while I've been away. I double click on the top one from Bristol police station.

ne9jam6aism1ou0b0li1es

Fats jumps up onto my bed, purring loudly, and tries to climb on my knee. I stare at the garbage. Then Fats plonks his big paw on the space bar and suddenly I see

ne9 jam6aism1ou0b0li1es

ne jamais stares out at me. Quickly I cut and paste the numbers onto the line below. Fats dabs playfully at my tapping fingers.

ne jamaismoublies

'Fats! You're amazing!' Fats must think I'm cross with him because he jumps down from the bed and stalks off, tail high. I hit the space bar again and stick in an apostrophe.

ne jamais m'oublies
Never Forget Me
N F M

I've broken three of the letters on that coded message. What were the other ones? I can remember CR, but not the first group.

I look at the numbers: **9 6 1 0 0 1**

Perhaps they're part of a mobile number, or an email address. I rack my brains but nothing's happening, so I phone a friend.

Becks' voice is sleepy. 'D'you know what time this is?'

'The message, Becks! Never Forget Me!'

'That's a cheesy excuse for waking me up in the middle of the night!'

'Get your brain into gear, Becks! DIW emailed me the original file name and Fats and I decoded it from the French. Never Forget Me is what the second group of letters stands for – N F M, remember?'

She yawns. 'Oh, right. … FATS … ?'

'But there are these numbers that were jumbled up with the file name … '

Her voice is resigned. 'Go on.'

'Nine, six, one, zero, zero, one.'

There's a pause and I think she's dozed off again. Then, 'My birthday.'

'What?'

'October 1st, 1996.' Becks is slowly waking up. 'The date of the email? Or some other date? Maybe the numbers got jumbled up with the message when it was sent … or maybe they were deliberately mixed up …'

'Becks – that's sixteen years ago! They didn't have email then.'

She's wide awake now. 'They did too! The Queen sent her first email in 1976.'

'How on earth do you know that random fact?'

'I know everything, get used to it. Point is, what are we looking at?'

'A message, Never Forget Me, sent by CR or to CR, and the date is 1st October 1996.'

'Can you remember the first group of letters?'

'Only a P and maybe an M or an H. I'll call DIW …'

'No, DON'T, Joe!'

'Why not? We could crack this and …'

'What if Monsieur's first name actually does begin with a C?'

'He wouldn't have sent the email to himself.'

'Exactly! So it's possible that this Pashmina woman sent it to him. And if we tell DIW what we know, he'll immediately assume that she and Monsieur are linked together in the drug running. Then he'll NEVER get off Monsieur's back!'

'If it WAS sent to Monsieur all that time ago, why is it still there? That computer in the underground room couldn't have been more than two years old.'

'Once Bertolini took over Monsieur's company, he would have controlled what was on the computer, too.'

'You think he knew about the file?'

'And kept it to blackmail Monsieur, to strengthen his hold over him. Another turn of the screw!'

I can hear the anger in Becks' voice. But there's another voice in my head now, quietly talking to me, behind a door that's slowly opening. 'Or, Monsieur was the one who kept it. And he put all that protection on it so that Bertolini couldn't access it, or delete it.'

'Why would he do that when it could link him to Pashmina?'

'BECAUSE it would link him to her … if … something happened to him.'

Becks' voice is a whisper. 'You think … she wanted to kill Monsieur?'

'Why else would he have kept it? He must have known how deadly she is.'

'But why would she want to kill him?'

'She poisons people who get in her way. And Monsieur was a Commander like my dad, wasn't he? He could have been working to bring her operation down but then it all went wrong with Arnaud and Bertolini.'

'But … after all this time?'

'Remember what DIW said? Some of the people she's poisoned have links with her that go back years. Maybe sixteen years.'

'But we don't know if she sent it to Monsieur because we don't know if his first name begins with a C.'

'I'm an idiot, Becks. I've been sitting on it.'

My hand goes to my back pocket, to that battered envelope with the remains of the Euros and fifty pound notes that Monsieur gave us. He'd written a brief message. But I never even looked at it, all those times that Monsieur's money saved our skins. Now at last, reproaching myself bitterly for ever having been angry with Monsieur, I read the elegant script:

My dear Joe,
In the hope that this may help you and Becks to keep safe.
With my love to you both,
Christian.

Becks says quietly, 'So it was sent to Monsieur. We have to warn him that we've seen her …'

'We need to warn him about something else, too.' I tell Becks about the hissed words at the airport.

'God, Joe. Do you think your dad has gone over to this woman's organisation?'

Both your father and I, for different reasons, became part of the very evil we were fighting.

The anger almost chokes me. 'Listen, Becks. If Commander Julius Grayling is working with this woman against Monsieur, then he isn't my father anymore!'